No Birds Sang

By the same author

HANGMAN'S TIDE

NO BIRDS SANG

JOHN BUXTON HILTON

ST. MARTIN'S
NEW YORK

© 1975 by John Buxton Hilton

All rights reserved. For information, write:
St. Martin's Press, Inc., 175 Fifth Ave., New York, N.Y. 10010

Library of Congress Catalog Card Number: 75-18720

First published in the United States of America in 1976

Printed in Great Britain

For
Elizabeth Adams

CHAPTER ONE

A livid slash in the bole of a twisted hawthorn where a recent bullet had torn away a triangle of bark; a signboard leaning on its side against a heap of crumbling bricks, sun-bleached and weather-cracked—the home-spun grace of a forelock-touching Edwardian tradesman: *Wm Penny, Supplier of Cattle Feeds and Farm Machinery*; a roof gaping open, rafterless and futile, against a concavity of empty sky.

Lance-corporal Taffy Davies squeezed the trigger and the Bren fired one round and stopped. He eased forward the barrel and called to Number Two to regulate the gas. Nine Platoon slithered forward on grass wet from a May shower. Rifle bullets cracked overhead like a cliché lick of whip-cord. From behind the gorse D Company put down their first smoke, twenty yards to windward of the target.

Number Two dropped his hand and fell back with parade ground self-consciousness. Davies fired a service-burst into the soft earth of a molehill. Then he saw the civilian's face, the panic gesture of an arm waving a white handkerchief in the gap that had once been a window. The smoke from the mortar bomb drifted across his field of vision and a second one came down with an earthy puff between the first burst and the corner of the cottage.

'*Corp!* There's somebody in there!'

The smoke was thickening now, both bombs belching orgiastically. From a flank an automatic rifle opened up, emptied half a magazine into the heart of their objective.

'Cease fire! Cease fire! There's a civvy in there!'

But some man at the extreme end of the section—Willoughby or Swann—had not heard, was just beginning to enjoy himself, was pumping single rifle shots willy-nilly into the smoke. Davies jumped to his feet.

'Cease fire, there!'

And from the rabbit hollow that was Platoon H.Q., Lieutenant Franklin was shouting in exasperated incomprehension.

'What the hell do you think you're on, Corporal? Get down man, get down! You're in Twelve Platoon's cross-fire. *Christ!*'

CHAPTER TWO

Derek Stammers lit a cheroot at the wheel and in the passenger-seat Kenworthy flexed his legs, eased his bottom and let the feeling of relaxation travel up his spine. Holidaying on another man's patch—he'd fought shy of it for years, and here it was, apparently working. Along the dead straight by-road the panorama of the trees was like an impressionist's palette, every gold, green and mother-earth brown in the pigment-box. And everything fresh, everything youthful. Ten minutes ago, it had rained; now the rogue cloud had passed elsewhere. Spring sunshine flooded the acres of wayside dandelion, hedge-parsley and ragged robin.

'And you get paid for this kind of motoring.'

'There are worse bailiwicks,' Stammers said. 'Yours, for example.'

'If you can call mine a manor.'

Then Stammers cocked up his eye quizzically at his mirror. An ambulance overtook them, blue lamp flashing, siren hysterical; seconds later an *Allegro* patrol-car, two tones of blue, doing at least ninety.

'Any policeman, of course, with a real taste for the charnel-house, gets into "Traffic". If it's along this stretch, Simon, I'd better stop and look. But I doubt if it'll be my pigeon.'

Three minutes later, they saw that it wasn't "Traffic". The ambulance was parked on the verge at the entrance to a forest ride; the panda car was behind it and there was a miscellany of military vehicles, a barbed wire barrier, a red range-flag and a guard-room compound.

'Trouble—for the army. But I'd better get myself informed.'

Derek got out, was about to slam the door, then looked back.

'Come if you want to, Simon, of course—'

Kenworthy smiled, lazy and affable.

'All yours, Derek.'

He lowered the window, looked idly out to where the ambulance drivers were off-loading a stretcher—and within five minutes was actually dozing. Once or twice within the next quarter of an hour he opened his eyes and was casually aware that something was happening: Red Caps arriving in a jeep, a tailor's dummy brigadier in a staff-car. The stretcher was put back empty into the ambulance and another one carried with reverence into the W.D. blood-wagon. The body's face was covered by the blanket. Kenworthy closed his eyes again. Derek was obviously going to be some little time. The ladies were waiting to be picked up for a hotel lunch; but policemen's wives were used to being patient. At least, Elspeth was. No doubt Derek had Diana equally well trained.

Then Derek came back through the trees, talking to a lieutenant-colonel and a captain.

'Simon—I promise I'm not dragging you into anything—but I'd like you to see this.'

So Kenworthy got out of the car, with no very strong feelings either way. He wasn't going to let himself get tied up—certainly he wasn't—but if Derek had something that he thought was curious, it was only polite to show an interest: like listening last night to the L.P.'s of the Welsh male voice choirs. The trouble about the brothers-in-law was that over the twenty-five years they had been acquainted, they had carefully avoided getting to know each other. Kenworthy was aware that he had a national reputation and suspected that Derek, in common with most of the senior men in provincial forces, was unimpressed. Derek, on the other hand, was known to be a bloody good country D.C.I.—and probably thought the world ended there.

They walked together between the trees, came to another barrier, another red flag, an armed sentry standing self-consciously regimental.

'A battle range, field training with live ammunition ...'

Kenworthy nodded vaguely. He was partially awake now, had almost involuntarily switched on his familiar, professional alertness, had started to look at passing faces and their expressions, had begun again, as on any working day in his life, the eternal vigilance for significant discrepancies. It had not come his way to have much to do with soldiers since 1946. These men looked young, self-satisfied, perhaps a shade more intelligent than he remembered the army, the N.C.O.s confident, the C.O. impatient.

'A man's been killed. It's bad for these others to be kept hanging about.'

They were a training battalion, practising platoon-in-the-attack. There was a metallic tang of cordite, alien to the spring morning. The mortar smoke had dissipated in wisps across the scrubland. A platoon was halted along the edge of a nursery pine plantation. The colonel played hell with a sergeant who had neglected to post a superfluous look-out, forgetting the rules of the war-game in the face of death itself.

'Give us twenty minutes,' Derek said. 'I want to look over the spot before you plaster it with H.E.'

'Waste of your time, Chief Inspector. The man's a simple trespasser.'

'A trespasser—but not so simple. This is the third time.'

The colonel conferred with his adjutant, then nodded his agreement. A Field Security Sergeant stepped forward from the band of satellites.

'May I come, too, please?'

'Of course. But I'll tell you now, you'll find nothing you won't write off.'

'All the same, sir.'

'I said *of course*, didn't I? Obviously you've never come across Milner.'

'No, sir.'

'How long have you been covering this district?'

'Six months.'

'And there's nothing about Milner on your files?'

'I don't know the files by heart, sir.'

Derek made no further comment. They set out through knee-deep vegetation: the yellow straggling weeds favoured by the sandy soil, the wiry brush of heather against their trousers. The gashed hawthorn stretched branches heavy with blossom, spreading like an arm towards the leeward southwest.

'Six square miles of it, give or take a rood or two. Requisitioned by the War Office in 1941, to teach the infantry what they ought to have been learning in the 1930s. Two villages involved—well, a village and a hamlet—Yarrow Cross and Pegg's Corner, in that order. The population was compulsorily rehoused, mostly in nearby town estates, but some went further afield. Smallholders were compensated: I don't know how well. Everybody took it that the area would be decontrolled as soon as the war was over but, as you can see, the M. of D. have held on. There's been a bit of fuss, sporadically, but it's mostly died down now. Nobody seems to care—except Milner. Now and then a picnic party strays accidentally, and has to be turned back by the standing patrol. There's a lot of unexploded ammo about—they say. Local poachers take their chances as they come, probably with the patrol's connivance. Once a year the barriers are lifted, and there's a day's free access to the church, between taped lanes. They have a service; I don't know who comes. Milner doesn't; he's not interested when he's allowed to be.'

They came to the first pile of overgrown rubble that marked the village's extremity. Self-sown saplings apparently found sustenance in the cracks between stones. A gorse-bush had taken root high on a remnant of wall.

'There's a caretaker skeleton unit always here. They put a few stones back in the intervals between assault courses—just to make sure there's something left to aim at.'

'And your man Milner used to live here?'

'Never in his life. Never within two hundred miles. He's never had any connection with the place that we've been able to unearth. But he keeps coming. That's why I thought he might interest you.'

Kenworthy did not ask questions. He would show the required interest, but he proposed to let the whole thing ride over him. He found the heath more than merely pleasant. It was the sort of place he thought he could revel in—for an hour or two: the hum of insects, an ecstatic lark, the forty shades of green. He vaguely liked the sort of speculation that was set up by a deserted village, the corner shop, the wreck of a vicarage. But he had no difficulty in allowing himself to be unaffected by recent sudden death. That was the point of a holiday: to be outside things.

The patch where the lance-corporal had died had been roped off with improvised stakes. There was a massive and glaring crimson stain on the bank. Blood had splashed grass and trees yards away from where the N.C.O. had spun round and fallen. His section had been marched back fifty yards and were sitting about, smoking cigarettes and talking unnaturally loudly. Most of them had not encountered death before.

Derek led into the ruin at which the section had been firing. Once a cottage, two up and two down, its ground-plan was piled deep in the debris of its roof-timbers. The door was off its hinges and a surprising number of trainees had found time to carve their initials, their home-towns and their football teams in woodwork and stone. Within the last hour a bullet had ricocheted from the window-sill: the single round before Lance-corporal Davies's stoppage.

The room in which he had spotted the intruder was choked

with rubbish and rubble: plaster, rotting beam-ends. Weeds were in command everywhere.

'We'll find nothing. But at least we can say we looked.'

Stammers picked up a cigarette end.

'Woodbine. One of Milner's economies. He's never smoked anything else. A very careful man, Milner.'

They picked their way through nettle-beds and over garden fences to a metalled road that had been the nuclear village street. Now, mangled by generations of tracked vehicles, there seemed almost as much random plant life amongst the broken asphalt as there was out in the eroding heathland. Buildings had stood up unevenly to the years of assault. Here and there a gable-end was discernible; in places a cluster of pantiles still sagged against an irrational remnant of roof-beam. Other habitations were no more than heaps of rubble, each in its own overgrown crater.

Derek knew them all.

'John and Wilfred Whittle—flint-knappers.'

'What's a flint-knapper?'

'Ancient trade, goes back before the Iron Age. Arrowheads, tools and, later, stones for building. I did hear that there are one or two still at it in Brandon. Apparently in some parts of Africa they still need chippings to fire their muskets. But I don't know what's happened to the Whittle family. I've lost touch. Where Milner was snooping was the Carvers' cottage. Over there the Parsons'. The big house was the Prudhoes'.'

They crossed the road, and Derek pointed to a Hanoverian facade, the ground-floor windows boarded up, part of the roof gone, and most of the ridge-tiles missing. It was set in parkland that had reverted to a reminder of savannah.

'Gentlemen farmers. Bought a place in Wiltshire on the proceeds of compulsory purchase. Probably the only ones in the village who made anything on the deal. God, I owe something to Milner, Simon. I never set foot in this place while a soul lived here; but there was a time when I knew its ins and outs as well as if I'd lived here half my life.

That's what the Milner file did for me. Let's go and talk to him. The very sight of him makes me feel sick.'

They trudged out to the rear of the Field H.Q., where the two uniformed constables from the patrol car were guarding their prisoner, unnecessarily supported by two private soldiers with fixed bayonets.

'You've done it this time, Milner.'

He was a man in his early fifties, fresh faced, cleanly shaven, extremely neatly dressed, though more nearly in the fashions of his own youth than following the trends of the century. His sports jacket, in fact, seemed to be new; the crease in his trousers was razor-edged, and except for a patch of scuffing against the stone, his brown shoes looked as if he polished them endlessly. He was wearing a stylish dark green felt hat, beneath which the trim of a fortnightly hair-cut was apparent. But someone had stuck a patch of plaster across his right cheek-bone, and there was a streak of grime across his forehead.

'You hurt, Milner?'

Milner did not raise his eyes. There was an old-fashioned discipline in his dress and deportment, and this seemed to go for his sense of shame, too.

'I said, are you hurt?'

'Just grazed. A chip of stone flew off the sill.'

'You stupid bastard.'

Milner did not defend himself.

'A man stood up to save your life and he's dead, Milner.'

Milner was like a domesticated animal, offering no excuses for a familiar offence.

'What can you expect me to say about it, officer?'

'He was a married man, Milner, with a child of two and another on the way.'

'I shall send them every penny I've got—even if I have to sell my own bed. And I know that won't do more than scratch the surface.'

He spoke with a perceptibly north country accent, but not aggressively so: a soft Lancashire burr; he gave the impression that his voice was mild by nature, perhaps even musical to listen to, when he was not under stress.

'Something like this was bound to happen sooner or later, Milner. I warned you last time. I only wish it was you they'd carted off ...'

'So do I. Do you think I'll ever get a night's sleep again?'

'Not on the sort of bed I'm going to try to fix for you. Because if there's a stretch to be got for you for this, Milner, I'm going to see you get it. And I doubt whether you'll find a solicitor with the nerve to ask for mitigation.'

'I shan't ask for any.'

Derek Stammers looked at Milner rancorously. Kenworthy knew the feeling. He'd let himself get personally involved in cases of his own in his time.

And Milner muttered something that neither of them caught.

'Say again, Milner.'

'I said, it doesn't matter now.'

'It matters to me—and you'll be lucky if it's left in my hands. And I don't care whether it is or it isn't, Milner. I'm going to get the truth out of you if I have to forget myself in the process.'

Stammers was letting his anger get out of control. Kenworthy felt both for and against him. A copper ought to know when it was a brick wall his head was bouncing off. And any real villain would be delighted to see the law succumbing to its own weaknesses.

But Milner continued to behave as if he were anything but a villain. He did not seem affected by the threats; his torment seemed to go genuinely deeper.

Stammers turned to his constables.

'Take him to hospital. Casualty ward.'

'I don't need a hospital,' Milner said. 'It's only a scratch.'

'Any scratch on you is going to get V.I.P. treatment, Milner. I'll make sure of preserving you. See what they say, Constable. I don't think they'll keep him, and if they don't, take him to Divisional H.Q. and detain him. Tell Detective-

Sergeant Pollitt to refresh himself from the files, and then start taking a statement. I'll be along sometime this afternoon to finish it.'

He looked challengingly at Milner. The adjutant approached.

'The C.O. ...'

'Yes. We're through.'

As they were getting back into Derek's car, they heard the soft thump of another smoke bomb. Number Two had presumably moved up to be Number One on the Bren.

CHAPTER THREE

'Sorry from two points of view,' Derek said. 'I shouldn't have let myself get carried away. And I shouldn't have given the impression that I normally do.'

He was still annoyed, translating his anger to some extent into his driving: he overtook a farm tractor with little to spare in face of an oncoming oil-tanker.

'Sorry, Simon.'

The hair's breadth seemed to sober him. He touched his foot-brake and brought their speed down to forty-five.

'I talk like that—and I know that the maximum fine is twenty quid. He got that last time: unauthorised entry on to Ministry of Defence property. It's all I can get him for. I know. I've tried. By the way, *does* he interest you?'

'I'm trying not to let him.'

'Sorry again, Simon. I promised both you and Elspeth ...'

But after another half mile, he started again.

'It was a couple of years after the war that I first came across Milner. I was a detective-constable. He was one of my first assignments after I came off the beat. He'd been picked up out there, charged with unauthorised entry. There wasn't a training programme on at the moment, so he wasn't personally at risk, nor was he jeopardising anybody else. He pleaded guilty, and didn't plead any extenuating circumstances. They fined him a fiver and kicked his arse out of it. In his statement, he said he fancied the look of the countryside, and as all was quiet, he'd stepped over the wire for a stroll. We took it at its face value. There was a lot of local feeling about the area, and the bench weren't entirely unsympathetic. If the patrol had just given him a gentle warning and sent him on his way, we'd all have been saved a lot of trouble.

'But there was a bit more to it than the public or the bench ever saw. We'd had to inform MI5 as a matter of routine; and you know what those buggers are, once they get a new card on the index. I had to answer a lot of questions that wouldn't otherwise have been asked. But the case died on us. Milner was as naive as he looked. And, after all, Yarrow Cross never had been a hot-bed of military secrets. Especially in 1947, there wasn't much to be learned there that the Home Guard couldn't have told a man. Milner went back to Lancashire, and even MI5 seemed satisfied.'

Stammers changed down for a T-junction.

'A couple of years later Milner was back, poking about in the old village. Again he'd chosen a quiet day, and he wasn't in anybody's way. But he ran into a picket of the maintenance unit and landed back in my basket. Why, why, why? Why had he travelled from his home, the other side of Manchester, with no visible reason to bring him into the county? No relatives here, no friends, no connections that we could establish. And you saw his style: disarming honesty. He went as far as admitting that he had a reason—but he said it was strictly personal. That was as far as we got: I sweated out two six-hour stints with him and hardly got him out of the courteously smiling stage. The MI bods sent two chaps down—and they got no further than I had. There *was* something. Milner didn't take the trouble to deny it. But it didn't lie in our line of country: he said that over and over again; if he told us, we wouldn't believe him; if we believed him, we wouldn't be interested. There's a devilish obstinacy about the man. I've often thought, when it comes to questioning, a suspect's only got to keep his nerve, and he's got you beat. Milner did keep his nerve. He didn't even forget his manners. He wasn't truculent, he wasn't crude, he didn't get het up. He just declined to talk.

'I was still a nobody on the case, anyway very junior; the operational decisions were not mine. While I was out on something else, a couple of the heavy lads visited his cell and roughed him up a bit. I don't know who; I could guess, but I didn't ask. Needless to say, it didn't work; it was the last thing on earth to do with a loner like that. It tightened him up more than ever—with a difference. Up to now he'd been thoroughly friendly—even when at his most uncooperative. Now he just turned everything off. But he didn't complain. Somehow, I'd known all along he wouldn't. It was still part of the price he was prepared to pay for something he was keeping to himself. Fined twenty quid—the maximum —and took a hell of a wigging from the bench that left him serenely unmoved.'

They were on a real main road now, jammed between lorries and unable to pull out into the centre lane.

'That's more than twenty years ago, Simon, and the bugger comes back for more.'

'Obviously, you put in a lot on the background.'

'The police in his home-town couldn't have been more helpful—or more knowledgeable. A well known character back home; very staid, very well dug in, very highly respected. Good record in the war-time R.A.F. We walked all round him many times. And to hear him apologise to the magistrates, for the trouble he'd caused—whilst paying his fine spot cash, all ready for them in new notes in a sealed envelope—you could understand why everybody called him a gentleman. Now, a quarter of a century later, he's nosing about in the same ruined cottage ...'

'Which you'll now have to dig over,' Kenworthy said quietly.

'That will be difficult. The military ...'

He stopped for traffic lights, negotiated the turning into town.

'Perhaps you'll be lucky,' Kenworthy said. 'Perhaps MI5 will take it right out of your hands, or at least turn it over to Special Branch.'

'Would you call that luck?'

'If anyone offers to take work off my hands, I don't complain.'

'You've outgrown letting cases matter to you, haven't you?'

Stammers manoeuvred them into the hotel carpark.

'No, but I've always regretted it when I've let it happen.'

Derek switched off the ignition, but paused for a moment before opening the door.

'I'd like to talk to you some more about this one, Simon, I'm convinced there's nothing in it for Special Branch.'

'Any time you like,' Kenworthy said. But he said it mechanically.

CHAPTER FOUR

They did not talk shop over lunch. Diana was clearly peeved that they were late, but she did not actually say anything. Elspeth was faintly amused by it. Derek went off alone for the afternoon, leaving Kenworthy to drive the women on a round trip of ruined priories. And then Derek was late home for supper, which made Diana privately very angry indeed, though she still kept up a semblance of outward aplomb. It was for ten minutes over the whisky, after the women had gone to bed, that the men had their first chance for anything but small talk.

'MI5 are interested, Simon, not to say pressing. Yet they

must *know* there's nothing on that range but outsize small-arms targets.'

'The odd weapon still on the classified list?'

Derek made guttural noises. 'Simon, you know as well as I do there's nothing there. And if you're looking for secret weapons, you don't go and stand in the firing-line. Besides, you've seen Milner. You've heard me talk to him. The man's not a spy. He's just a sodding nuisance. But you know the law: if we can pin on him a suggestion of undesirable contacts, the face of the case changes. Otherwise it's unauthorised entry again; there is a charge in the book, interfering with manoeuvres, but the max for that is even less.'

'So. He's a sodding nuisance. He's an even bigger nuisance uncleared on MI5's books than he is on yours. So what are they going to do about him?'

'Leave him to us; but they've asked for a daily run-down. Which means three or four times as much work. Also they want him held.'

'Should be easy.'

'On a charge as trivial as this? Fortunately, he's played into our hands.'

He replenished Kenworthy's glass with as much whisky as he normally drank in a fortnight.

'Fortunately, the hospital diagnosed delayed shock. They're keeping him overnight. Wouldn't let us near him; but I know the consultant well enough to lift a corner of professional ethics. And there's no doubt that Milner's undergoing a man-size ration of remorse. Talking of going to see the corporal's widow the moment he's discharged. Well, that won't be for a few days. I'm hoping for an Emergency Order under the Mental Health Act. That'll give us seventy-two hours: extendible to twenty-eight days, with a bit of co-operation.'

'Dangerous,' Kenworthy said.

'Oh, I don't know, suicidal tendencies.'

'I don't mean that. You can get him held if you want to. But you'll lose him in a trick-cyclist's paradise.'

'I've got a trick-cyclist I can trust,' Stammers said.
'That'll be the day.'
'No, really, Simon. I've worked with this chap off and on for years.'
'Sorry. You know your own manor.'

Play it careful; Kenworthy was not yet convinced that holidaying with in-laws made sense. He yawned. Elspeth had spent some of the best hours of their lives waiting for him to come to bed.

He found her sitting up against the pillow, reading in fits and starts, trying to keep herself awake for him. She was wearing a nightie that she had made specially for this holiday. Her arms were smooth; her skin could have been an advertisement for an admass super-soap. That was the point of a holiday. There was time, at least there ought to be, to look at each other a second time; time to relish that for a day or two the pressures were off; that tomorrow was going to be as fallow as today had been.

'Simon.'
'Darling?'
'Please don't let Derek think that you're half a step ahead of him.'
'I don't. Because I'm not. And he and I don't think that way. Have I said something that I shouldn't?'
'Of course not.'
'Has Derek said anything?'
'Far from it.'
'Diana, then?'
'She hasn't *said* anything.'
'I know. That's why I'm playing it careful.'

He got into bed. She turned her back to him, snuggled down on to his knees, moulded her body to his.

'Simon.'
'Darling?'
'Derek has been on a case today, hasn't he?'
'He's on a case every day. Several, as a rule.'
'Diana was telling me.'

'Uh-huh?'

'About this man Milner. How he's caused trouble for years, and now a man killed.'

'Derek has it well in hand.'

'I think he might rather like your help, you know.'

'We agreed, didn't we, that I wasn't even going to ...'

He put an arm round her.

'Simon.'

'Beloved?'

'I know we're on holiday. And I know what we said before we started. But I've caught sight of your face several times today. I don't know how you're going to tolerate a week without a job to do.'

'I had thought of trying. We might even find some more priories, if we look hard enough.'

'That's what I mean, Simon. If Derek does ask you—asks you direct, I mean—there's no need to go fishing for work. What I'm trying to say is this, Simon: if Derek does ask you, outright, there's no need to say no on my account.'

'I'll bear that in mind, but I'd probably say no on my own account, anyway.'

'There you are, you see, only *probably*. You see, I'm trying to make a condition, Simon.'

'Oh?' He began to wish she would go to sleep.

'This is my holiday too, and I can be as unofficial as you can.'

'Thus spoke the oracle. Interpreter, please.'

'If you do a case over Derek's shoulder, I'd like to be in on it with you.'

'We'll ask the Chief Constable.'

'Seriously, Simon. I don't mean come out and sit in on interviews. I mean stay abreast, move for move, just for once. Make it *our* holiday case.'

'Uh-huh.'

CHAPTER FIVE

They breakfasted late the next morning to enable Diana to get Derek away and give her a breathing space. She was an assiduous hostess. She was a woman who obviously suffered her frustrations, but she did manage to recognise, at least for most of the time, that these were not the fault of her guests. Her guests, therefore, she treated generally with a good grace, though not always with bounding cheerfulness. And her cheerfulness, when apparent, did sometimes look like a dutiful after-thought. Simon and Elspeth soon learned that it was easier to keep her mind off its own dark louring by-ways if they stayed well away from police matters in words and innuendo.

But after they had eaten, she handed Simon two files that were lying on the sideboard.

'Derek said you might care to look through these. But only if you want to. I must say, I think he has a nerve.'

'I'll have a few minutes with them.'

'He'll be home to lunch. He hopes. And he'll try to get an hour or two off this afternoon. He hopes.' Diana turned to Elspeth. 'Does Simon ever keep an appointment that he's made with *you*?'

'He isn't often within a fifty-mile radius. We have most of our fun on the phone. And I have one of the finest sets of picture-postcards in the country. Usually small town High Streets where someone or other felt something go snap in his head.'

'I wonder how much longer before something goes snap in mine.'

Simon retired into the other room with the papers. And he had not leafed through many pages before he acknowledged that there was someone in the force in the Lancashire borough of Ormisher Bridge who enjoyed letting himself go with a typewriter. Perhaps the fact that carbon copies of much of this had been destined for Military Intelligence had had some astringent effect on concentration and composition. The United Kingdom police station does not keep written records about people who have no criminal history: but it is often remarkable how much is known about some local characters when information is discreetly pooled.

And it was evident that Milner was a character in Ormisher Bridge: a drinking companion on occasion with all ranks from the Chief Superintendent down.

Edward Garstang Milner had been born in a cotton-spinning village not many miles from Bolton, of parents, now both deceased, who had lived and worked in that jealously preserved borderbelt between upper working and lower middle class. He had won a scholarship to an unsung, but solidly productive grammar school, which he had left at the end of his fifth year, with examination results that would have justified at least another couple of years' study. He had had no difficulty in finding himself a job in the Ormisher Bridge Town Hall, where he had become a costing clerk in the Borough Engineer's department. In the first autumn of the war he had volunteered for the R.A.F., had trained in South Africa, and, failing to qualify as a pilot (he had badly muffed several test landings), he had ended up as a Flight-Sergeant airgunner with Bomber Command.

There was official bumf from service records: an immaculate conduct sheet. They had dug out a report from one of his wing leaders: he had been in one or two operational near-misses—a wing-and-prayer home-coming more than once, half his turret shot away on one occasion. Once, twenty miles short of their base in Bedfordshire, he had survived a belly-flop landing. After demobilisation he had returned at once to Ormisher Bridge; had quietly and efficiently worked for professional examinations, and had advanced himself as far as Borough Engineer's Chief Clerk, being regularly (and safely) entrusted with responsibilities far in excess of his paper qualifications.

There was no history of anything to do with women. He did not seem interested. And yet the MI man who had talked to him after the second trespass had categorically recorded him as *not a queer*. Kenworthy could picture him losing his men-friends as they married themselves off one at a time. He was often away at weekends, but if there was any female interest in them, he kept it strictly, and successfully, away from Ormisher Bridge. In the 1950s he had moved himself from comfortable digs to a fairly expensive bachelor flat in a block that had been put up in one of Ormisher Bridge's development schemes. There he did his own housekeeping, his own evening cooking and his own cleaning: he was—the authority for this was, again, the security man—almost pathologically tidy. He treated his household as he treated his clothes; nothing must be out of place; everything looked remarkably new all the time.

And that, Kenworthy reflected, was probably how he treated people, too.

In his spare time, Milner was an active man. He fished in Ribblesdale, not by any means an exclusive or expensive stretch, which accounted for at least some of his weekends. He was a competent club-cricketer, and up to his mid-forties had still been going in number five for the Ormisher Bridge Second Eleven. He rarely took long holidays, but commuted his leave so as to see at least two days' play in most test matches. He knew his way about Lords and the Oval, Trent Bridge, Headingly, Old Trafford and Edgbaston. He was a moderate and regular beer drinker, rarely missed the last hour in the Ormisher Bridge *Bull*; stood his corner, was always good-natured in his cups. He was a very popular member of the town's top male ale drinking circle: the editor of the local paper, professional men, senior policemen out of uniform.

On balance, if I were reporting on this man other than in the present context, I would have no hesitation in recom-

mending him for high grade clearance.

That was an astonishing, almost fool-hardy comment for a security man to have committed to paper.

Kenworthy went into the kitchen, where Elspeth, having helped with the washing up, had left Diana to her mid-morning chores.

'Do you have an atlas, Diana? Something with southern England and a bit of the continental coast?'

Wiping her hands, she went to the bookcase and found him what he wanted, without making any conversation. When Elspeth came down and joined him, having rounded up their bedroom into faultless order, he was running his finger along the edge of a sheet of paper that he had laid across the map.

'May I be kept abreast of developments, please?'

'Just guessing.'

'I'm supposed to be working with you on this case. Remember? No secrets from me on this one.'

'When I'm out on a ploy, my sergeant knows better than to question me about my guesswork. It's one of the first things he has to learn.'

'I'm not a sergeant. We're both Chief Superintendents.'

'Too much rank about, for a case with only a twenty pound fine at the end of it.'

Elspeth smiled sweetly.

'Two Chief Superintendents, or no case.'

Kenworthy pointed down at the south-west corner of his paper.

'Just guessing. I must insist on that. And on the job I'm guessing all day long. Nine out of ten of my ideas are just plain barmy: but they do sometimes serve to get me going.'

'Simon, I haven't been married to you since 1941 without becoming aware of your haphazard methods.'

'This,' Kenworthy said, wriggling his finger, 'is one of Milner's wartime stations. In Bedfordshire. This is the area, twenty miles from home, where he crash-landed in a turnip field. This is a straight—or straightish—line from those two places, crossing the long deserted battle village of Yarrow Cross and the battle hamlet of Pegg's Cross. Continue along the line of the sheet, not allowing too much for drift, or a dicey rudder, or one engine gone, and you've come out across the Dutch coast, a little north of Amsterdam. A favourite mustering point for returning sorties.'

'Um. We *are* guessing, aren't we?'

'I said so. But it isn't as remote as you might think, Elspeth. Look at it this way: if he wants to go to Yarrow Cross because of something someone's told him about the place, then this theory's plain duff. It isn't ruled out that he might have visited rural Norfolk as a boy; but it isn't likely that it wouldn't have come out if he had. On the other hand, when he was stationed in the Home Counties, he must have flown operationally over the place dozens of times: a direct line to a rendezvous or dispersal point over Great Yarmouth. We have reasonable evidence that he once came in over there, low and slow.'

'You do get carried away, don't you? Is this how we solve all our cases?'

'Look: all I'm giving you is a line of constructive speculation.'

'I know, I know, I'm with you. Don't you know when your leg's being pulled?'

'So when I see Master Milner—*if* I see Master Milner—one of the things I shall ask him, at least, I won't ask him I'll let him see that I presume ...'

Elspeth looked wistful.

'I wish I could sit in on you and Master Milner.'

'That, I'm afraid, my dear ... God, I don't know what Derek would say to that.'

At which moment Diana came in with coffee for them, caught the last remark, and evidently put some construction on it that she did not much like. The Kenworthys saw her eyes cloud momentarily; but neither of them felt equal to the complexity of explaining to her.

'You'll excuse me for a quarter of an hour? I must pop down to the shops.'

Kenworthy passed Elspeth the file on Milner and picked up the second one himself. It contained a pre-war map of part of the training area, six inches to the mile, and with each of the habitations neatly numbered in red ink. He had no difficulty in orientating himself from the side-road down which Derek had driven him. But it was not so easy to know which was the cottage in which Milner had been trapped by the corporal's fire. There were noticeably more houses on the map than there had seemed to be on the ground. Presumably many had succumbed altogether to blast and direct hits. Perhaps fire had swept parts of the site more than once. One terrace of cottages was marked in a place where he remembered seeing nothing but weeds.

He decided the one he was looking for was No. 27: and in the lists that were appended—the last electoral roll of the village ever to be compiled—its occupants were glossed as Carver, John and Carver, Emily Jane. That was the name that Derek had mentioned. But it was not possible, from Kenworthy's hasty memory of the terrain, to be sure of the relationship with other dwellings.

Some of the families were easy to spot. The vicarage was plain enough: the Rev. Wilfred Paish and his wife, with evidently his wife's mother or an aunt, and two grown-up off-spring (minors were not included). And there was Yarrow Cross Hall: Richard John Prudhoe; no one else of the same name in the house, but several other surnames: retainers, perhaps. There were Whittles all over the place: clearly not all flint-knappers.

And after the electoral roll there were typewritten sheets showing the immediate destinations of residents after the area had been cleared. Some attempt had been made to bring this up to date, presumably in the furore after Milner's second offence. This time only about two thirds of the villagers seemed to have been accounted for. More than twenty of them had died; most of those who could be traced had been settled, as Derek had said, in neighbouring towns. The Prudhoes had gone to Wiltshire. Kenworthy noted their address. It might be useful for consultation.

Elspeth looked up from her dossier.

'May I start guessing, too?'

'I won't ask more questions than a well trained sergeant.'

'He's frightened of women.'

'You think so?'

'There are men like that. They seem born to be bachelors. In later middle age they become very lonely. But it isn't that they don't like women. My uncle, James Cobbold, was engaged for twenty-three years. It was a family joke. Everybody knew they never would get married, nobody more realistically than the poor woman herself. Uncle James's ingenuity at putting it off was never ending. He was frightened of his own inadequacy, just couldn't face up to it. When *I* see Mr Milner ...'

'Elspeth, we've got to be realistic about this. I don't want to rattle the foundations of this partnership, but just how do you think we could arrange a session for you with Milner?'

'You're always swearing about people who have no imagination, Simon. Didn't you say he wasn't in prison, he's in hospital? And don't hospitals get a lot of casual visitors?'

'He's in hospital under pretty tight surveillance. And you couldn't ask Derek.'

'Derek won't frustrate me. Don't forget he is my baby brother. I was twisting him round my little finger before you'd even seen the digit.'

'But darling, Derek ...'

But it seemed they could not mention the man's name without causing Diana to materialise.

'What are you laying in store for Derek now?' she asked. She tried to sound casual about it, but only partially succeeded.

CHAPTER SIX

Derek was only a quarter of an hour late for lunch. Diana said it was something to have his company at midday, anyway, on two consecutive days. She did not add that it was a pity they did not have visitors every day; there was no need for her actually to say it.

Derek did not ask at table whether Simon had read the files. He did not keep entirely away from shop-talk, but confined himself to the morning's lightweights: a detective-sergeant's informant who had settled for fifty pence after asking twenty pounds for something they already knew. This led Kenworthy into a reminiscence of his own, a long and reasonably funny anecdote which did at least neutralise the conversation. Diana looked as if she was going to be bored to screaming point, but eventually weighed in with a smile that could have been spontaneous.

Derek had time for a cigar, half-an-hour's feet up with the newspaper and a round with the lawn-mower. He had an appointment at the hospital at three.

'Want to come and meet my tame head-shrinker?'

'I'd love to,' Kenworthy said, and saw that Elspeth was staring meaningfully at him. God, was she taking this seriously?

Derek saw it, too. 'Why don't you come for the ride? The place is set in rather splendid grounds, you could have a pleasant hour ambling round while we are talking.'

And as he drove, he talked about his co-operative consultant.

'He's done us a good turn more than once in the last ten years. There's no head-in-the-clouds about Menschel. He recognises that not so deep under the psychologist's jargon there does sometimes lie something as simple as a straightforward wrong'un. And a villain on Menschel's patch doesn't get an all-purpose Freudian permit to operate. "This man knows right from wrong," I've heard him say. "And he's opted for wrong because he's gambling on quick returns. Therefore he belongs to you and not to me." It'll be interesting to see what he's made of Milner.'

Menschel was a slightly built, nimble Central European Jew in his late thirties. On his desk was a framed photograph of his family, as well as a folded stethoscope. Derek went straight to what was evidently their key phrase.

'Well? Is he yours or mine?'

'Neither.' Menschel had an impish smile that concealed a strong will. 'He has committed an amoral and calculated misdemeanour. But as to mind and emotion, he is as soundly in control as you or I.'

'Oh.'

Menschel's accent bore slight traces of his polyglot origins. It came out most strongly when he was being consciously colloquial.

'Oh, I don't mind giving him the benefit of our hotel facilities for a day or two. Let him rest up after a harrowing experience. Likewise your extremely keen day- and night-watchmen: they look as if they could do with a break. But I don't know why you're wasting man-power like this. Why not just get him to give you his word? He's far too sentimental to break it. Anyway, another day, two more perhaps, but there can be no question of our keeping him here indefinitely, or even for very long.'

'I see. Well I don't think that need give us any problem. He can pay his fine and go home. Just so long as I can write in a satisfactory explanation of the fatal attraction of Yarrow Cross Heath.'

'I doubt very much whether you'll be able to do that.'

'Surely that's the key to his personal difficulties?'

'Personal difficulties? I'm not particularly impressed by his personal difficulties. They're no greater than my own, or even yours, probably. He has his uncertainties, if you like, but who hasn't? If Milner were God Almighty in his Heaven, there are certain things about him that he'd order rather differently. But he has no difficulty in facing up to things as they are. In fact, I'd say he's coping rather magnificently. Oh, Mr Kenworthy, please do smoke if you want to.'

He had spotted that Kenworthy's hand was fidgeting in the direction of his jacket pocket.

'What you're saying,' Derek said, 'is that you have indeed found something out, and that you're not going to tell us?'

Menschel thought very carefully about his words. 'Yes: I think that is a fair statement of the situation.'

'Professional ethics? You're throwing the book at us? I have to respect you, of course, but you haven't always been so insistent.'

'It isn't a question of professional ethics. You know me, Chief Inspector. I try to do what seems right in the individual instance.'

He followed this by a short silence. Kenworthy could see that the man's decision was firm, and he hoped that Derek was not going to waste time and effort on it.

Derek, however, seemed to be of the same mind. He simply nodded. 'I'm beaten, then.'

'Not at all. All you have to do is go away and forget all about Edward Milner. Believe me, I know all about him, at least I know about all that concerns these unfortunate episodes on the battle range. And I can give you my assurance there is nothing there that need concern you.'

'That's all very well from my point of view. I have no difficulty in believing you. But it won't do for the machine I work for.'

'Oh, blast the machine you work for!' Menschel's accent came over very strongly indeed.

'And blast the machine you work for, Doctor.'

Menschel smiled. 'It isn't a machine. I am working for Edward Milner. And if I betray him to you—this is not being sententious, I think it is the right word in the circumstances—he would have no more confidence in my profession for the rest of his life. And that would be a pity. Perhaps even, if ever he needed our help, a very real danger.'

'But why will he tell you and not me?'

'Because he is a shy man, and does not expect you to make allowances for him. Because, like so many shy men, he will put a great deal of energy into defending some very simple stance. Because he does not care to look foolish. And you would think him very foolish, Chief Inspector.'

'I think he's a pestilential nuisance.'

Menschel laughed. 'Aren't we all, to someone?'

'May I talk to him, discreetly?'

'Of course. Though I have to make a condition.'

'You'd want one of your colleagues present?'

'Not that. I would trust you, Mr Stammers, of course I would trust you. But there is one topic I would ask you not to mention.'

'The one I've come to mention, I suppose.'

'I don't mean that one, Mr Stammers. A man is dead. You are very sorry about that, and angry. I am sorry about it, too, but not angry, because I am at a stage more remote than you from what was after all an accident. Edward Milner is sorry and very angry with himself. He does not yet see it as an accident. But he is beginning to already, which may save him from a very harmful guilt-complex. I am not interested in the morals of this issue, merely in its avoidable effects on an individual. So please don't try to use it as an emotional lever to make him talk about other things. Edward Milner will for the rest of his life be sorry for what he caused. But he has to try to accommodate it as a hard fact. It would be a pity if you started playing devil's advocate with his conscience at this delicate juncture. You'll find him somewhere in the grounds, Mr Stammers, and your day-watchman hovering on his horizon. We haven't put either of them in a padded cell.'

Kenworthy and Stammers climbed from the slow crunch of a gravelled drive to the swell of a closely mown bank. Rhododendrons were in full flower. The garden behind the main body of the hospital wound away into an oblivion of vegetation that looked almost dark in its distant shadows.

'What do you make of that?' Derek asked.

'I think Menschel's right,' Kenworthy said. 'All along the line he's frustratingly right. I can talk as serenely as that about it because this isn't my case. If it were, I'd be fuming.'

'I suppose ...' Derek hesitated.

'You were going to ask me something?'

'You wouldn't care to have a go at Milner?'

'If you like.'

'Any approach I make is buggered from the start by last time's failure. Plus the fact that he'll connect me with another round of rough stuff.'

'We've got to find him first.'

The grounds were not perhaps as extensive as they seemed at first sight: perhaps about five acres in all, but given a magic dimension by the variety of the landscaping and by the contours that led seemingly endlessly from one surprising vista to another.

'Could do with a spell in here myself,' Kenworthy said.

They came upon Milner and Elspeth sitting together on a bench under a Lebanon cedar, a tree so old that its lower branches, extending almost to ground level, were propped up by old railway sleepers. Quite forty yards away, on another bench, a plain-clothes man was reading a paperback. Simon and Derek approached them obliquely from behind.

'I think I'll saunter back through the woods, Simon. I've got some paperwork in the car I can be getting on with. Don't hurry.'

Kenworthy went on alone: and after only a few more yards across the springy turf, he emerged from the couple's blind spot. Milner sprang up at once when he saw him.

It was obvious immediately that though they could not have been talking for much more than half-an-hour, Elspeth and Milner had taken to each other. He was wearing the same clothes as yesterday: immaculate. Somebody must have worked hard on his white nylon shirt. And there was a much smaller strip of plaster, a mere speck, on his cheek instead of the rough old length that some medical orderly had billposted on him yesterday. He was smiling: Elspeth had a way with shy people, if she liked them, which she usually did. She said that reserve usually concealed something worth finding.

Elspeth was smiling, too, and looking very smart. That was another thing that holidays were for—noticing what your wife was wearing. It was her first summery costume after the winter, though not in the print-dress stage yet: there was still too much threat of chilliness in the season. A two-piece in powder-blue that did justice to her figure; she did not look a day older than thirty-five. And she, too, stood up as Simon approached and formally introduced the two men. Kenworthy reflected that he had made initial approaches to suspected persons in a variety of ways: but this made history.

Milner knew him as the subject of newspaper reports, of course, and made the right sort of remark, without being fulsome or—as was more usually the case—painfully comic. And then he looked at Elspeth as if asking for guidance as to how the conversation ought to continue.

'Mr Milner has been telling me a lot of things that you need to know and that won't bother you very much, Simon, once you know them.'

Kenworthy sat down on the end of the bench with Elspeth between them. Milner hesitated to make a start.

'You don't have to worry about talking in front of my husband, Mr Milner. He *does* need to know and he is the most sympathetic of listeners.'

'Oh, yes, I'm not fighting shy of telling him. I wish he had been around years ago, so I could have told him then. It's starting again for the second time within a few minutes that I find a little embarrassing.'

'You've no need to, Mr Milner. Really, you've no need to be embarrassed.'

'Of course I haven't. Silly of me.'

Milner made himself begin, talking rather fast at first as he played his way into his story.

'It was in the war. Early 1941. Only a matter of months—not all that many weeks—before these people were forcibly turned out of Yarrow Cross. I was a Flight-Sergeant air-gunner at the time: *Tail-end Charlie*, to give me all my proper dues.'

Arse-end Charlie, Kenworthy thought. But it was the hallmark of Milner not to use that sort of talk in front of a woman.

'It was quite a legendary role, wasn't it, that of airgunner? Especially a rear gunner, because he was a long way out behind. I don't know whether statistics did prove that airgunners had a lower expectation than any other form of animal life in the clouds. I think it was the usual manner of our going that used to impress people. Sometimes, *Tail-end Charlie* was the only one who bought it; and sometimes his mates didn't know for certain till they'd landed whether he'd bought it or not. He was all on his own: and the inter-com was brewed up even more often than the bloke in the turret.

'I know this sounds like a long preamble, but I must ask you to put up with it. It's the only way to give you the real flavour of it. We chaps, you know, we didn't get blasé, even if we tried to make it look that way. And it didn't get better with experience: it got worse. I had half my turret shot away once—the perspex, that is. I could feel the slip-stream pulling me out. I wrapped my legs round the gun-base till I'd practically tied knots in myself. And one phrase only kept wandering round my brain: "Milner, if you let go of that gun, you've had it".'

A saltier expression, of course; but not with a lady present.

'I never had a direct hit. Only ricochets.' He put his hand to his cheek with a mournful grin. 'I seem prone to catch flying chips. But it wasn't the things that hit you that were the trouble. It was the ones you were expecting. And it wasn't just what was happening in and round your turret: it was what you could hear and imagine happening to the rest of the kite. Flak through the fuselage. A wallop on the wing, and you wondered if that was an elevator-flap gone. You could read a disaster into a change of engine-sound.'

'I feel like that as a passenger on a Trident,' Kenworthy said.

'And one night stands out. We'd taken a gash or two on our way to Germany, but it was the barrage over Holland on the way home that did the damage. We must have had three direct hits, and the navigator had already put one fire out. If it had happened before the bomb went, we shouldn't be sitting here under these trees. We'd lost a starboard engine, too. And I was stuck back there, piecing it together from the sound-track. Bucketing and juddering. How much fuel had we lost? Remember I was travelling backwards, being dragged through an early dawn. It was rather like sitting astride a log that's being pulled over loose boulders.

'It was one of those gorgeous nights in late spring when it never gets wholly dark. The whole world, whether it was Nazi Europe or pastoral Norfolk, was held in a thin mist. It would clear in patches as soon as the sun began to make itself really felt.'

The spot in which they were sitting was equally at odds with his narrative. A red squirrel, there are not many left in East Anglia, came scurrying down the trunk of a beech and scampered away across the grass.

'I knew we were over the North Sea. I knew we'd lost height. I didn't know how much. I couldn't tell mist from water. Then suddenly we'd crossed the coast. I didn't see the actual moment of it, but suddenly I saw a new kind of surf down there: not sea this time, the tops of trees. Fresh green, breaking buds, only it still wasn't quite light enough to get the full colour of it, and the mist was still coming up in pillars. All I knew was those trees were too damned near. I could feel the struggle going on up front, Barney Fitzgerald and Alan Lucken, hauling with main force on the control column, trying to lift us with sheer physical strength bursting out of their chests.

'But lift us was the one thing they couldn't do. We bumped up once, on a thermal, but we were down the next second.

You know what an air-pocket does to you? One sudden lift-shaft drop of fifty feet would ground and splinter us, chuck bits of spar and fabric over a half-mile radius. Something slapped against the perspex, only it wasn't shrapnel this time. It was a twig. It could have been enough to tip us off what axis we had left. We were lucky that time: next time it might not be a handful of leaves.'

The squirrel picked up a morsel of last year's mast, examined it and threw it scornfully to one side.

'I didn't want to die, by God, I didn't want to die. That was a lovely dawn. I wanted to see others like it.

'It was better for them up front. They could see what was happening. They were still trying to do something about it.

'I tried to school myself to it. I just wasn't ready for it. Would I know anything about it when it happened? They weren't just prayers I said: I was trying to get hold of God himself.

'Then suddenly we'd cleared the trees. It was the edge of Yarrow Cross, slightly askew. And I was looking down on a receding cottage, not ten feet to spare, if that. And there was a girl in an upstairs window, sitting out on the sill, her hair long and wild, her breasts barely covered by her nightdress. She wasn't expecting visitors, was she, at that time in the morning? Especially not from the sky.

'She'd be sixteen or seventeen, I supposed, a woman already—unspoiled.'

He smiled expectantly at Simon and Elspeth. 'People don't talk like that any more, do they? Well, I'm going to say quite a few other things that don't belong to the 1970s. She looked up at me, and she waved, and I waved back. And, I make no bones about it, I bloody well cried. I remember nearly taking the skin off my eyes on the back of my flying-glove.'

His eyes were beginning to smart again as he told it; you could see that.

'I'll be honestly sentimental—she meant life to me, *my* life. She meant England. And that isn't contemporary talk, either, is it? Then she was gone. I don't know what speed we were down to, but I can't have been looking down at her for more than a few seconds. Then ...'

He smiled with a conscious sense of anti-climax. 'The village was sweeping backwards under us. I could see cottage gardens, ramshackle home-made sheds, bean-poles with nothing growing up them yet. I saw the big house, across its little park, columns of mist like giant men in front of those square windows. And then—I've never been so near to the face of a church clock in my life. Seventeen minutes to five, those hands stood at. I remember desperately trying to work out whether it had stopped or not. I still don't know.

'We were away from Yarrow Cross in no time, back over trees again. But somehow I wasn't so scared. I knew Barney and Alan would have a shot at putting us down on the first bit of flat they saw. And nine or ten minutes later, they did. I was concussed. When I came to, I was still looking at that girl in the window. Only she turned out to be a nurse saying "Hullo" as if she'd met me on a date by the station guard-room. They kept me in there a week or more. I was the only one of the crew to survive, which is why I'm a bit weak on some of the supporting detail.'

Something disturbed the squirrel. It ran helter-skelter to the nearest tree, shot up the trunk along a branch, leaped a gap across into a sycamore.

'So you came back to Yarrow Cross at your first opportunity?'

'First opportunity? When they let me out of that hospital, I went straight home. And then they posted me. When I first came back to Yarrow Cross, the roofs were off and the barbed wire was up.'

'What had you hoped to find? *Her?*'

'I knew I wouldn't. It was all of five years. I don't know. I just felt I had to see the place again, and was fined five quid for my pains. Do you think they'd have let me off with a caution if I'd told them I was chasing the image of a hand-wave?'

'It would have paid off,' Kenworthy said.

'I can see that now. But you weren't there, Mr Kenworthy. And your good lady wife wasn't there. And it was all so ... so *public*. It would have ruined my own memory, wouldn't it? And they seemed to think I was on the brink of some sort of sedition.'

Kenworthy answered him very quietly. 'You can't blame them for wondering.'

'Well, of course ...'

'Not *of course* in theory, Mr Milner, *of course* in fact. And that's what they're thinking now.'

Milner laughed, a short, unheartfelt chuckle. There was no optimism in it: it came from whatever drugs they had been feeding him.

'Absurd as it is ...'

'I wouldn't call it absurd. Or, at least, I think you should see it from the point of view of a group of by no means antagonistic policemen, well meaning, sympathetic souls, who ask no more than occasionally to see something go right for somebody.' God, he felt hypocritical; was he just playing up to Elspeth?

'By no means antagonistic ...' Milner started.

'Yes, I know, Milner, don't say it. Just don't say it. We can't just go to our superiors and say, "All right. It's absurd. I feel it in my bones. Close the file on my say-so." The men we know are being watched by men we don't know.'

'I can see that.'

'In that case ...' Kenworthy knew he had to do it; it was difficult in front of Elspeth. 'In that case, Milner, I suggest you tell us why you're really so anxious to keep going back to that damned heath.'

He'd tried to do it without that chop of hardness in his voice, had changed his mind in mid-sentence; realised he'd foozled it by any standard of interrogation.

But Milner certainly looked as if he got the message.

And Elspeth was too disciplined to let her facial expression change. It would be inexact to say that the smile froze on her face. The smile remained; she was urgently struggling still to give Milner confidence; but at the same time, she was as shaken by the change in Simon's tone as Milner was. For an instant all emotional interchange hung fire. For a moment Milner looked as if he were about to speak; his lips moved slightly, then no words came.

'Because, Milner, there *is* another reason. And I've no doubt it is as innocuous and innocent as the one you've just given us.'

Milner's mouth moved again. 'As a matter of fact ...'

But at that moment bodies came through the trees, crepe soles on the resilient turf, spring grasses brushing against the turn-ups of trousers. It was Menschel, accompanied by a male nurse in a white coat: a deceptively smiling man, with freckles, broad shoulders and a familiarity with hysterics.

'That'll have to do, Mr Kenworthy. Time for your medicine, Edward.'

The attendant had a medicine-cup containing small white pills, concealed like a conjuror in the palm of his hand.

'Tomorrow, perhaps?' Kenworthy said.

'I'll make no promises. One long talk, such as you've just had, yes. But it takes longer to forget than to remember. Another three or four days, perhaps.'

'But ...' Milner said.

'Now, Edward, you know what I told you: don't let them make you think it matters. Sorry, Mr Kenworthy, he *has* had enough.'

They led Milner away, up a bank between blossoming variegated brooms. And when they reached the car, Kenworthy let Elspeth tell the story to Derek.

Derek held them poised on the white line of a roundabout, fell in behind a mobile cement-mixer, and spoke again after he had pulled them out into their road home. 'And it's good enough for you?'

The question was addressed to Kenworthy.

'I do believe him.'

'I don't think I do,' Derek said.

'There are plenty of objections. It would be as well to run over them.'

'What speed could a plane like that drop to and still remain airborne? Eighty-five? I'm only guessing. I'm absolutely clueless on the point. But too damned fast, anyway, for human features to register. Especially a face that suddenly appears after an eternity of tree-tops and clouds.'

Derek suddenly put his foot down. The road ahead was clear. Some two hundred yards ahead of them a woman was pushing a pram. They passed her with the needle on a tremulous and dutiful seventy.

'We were looking for her and at her, and approaching her head on. What can you remember?'

'Not relevant,' Kenworthy said.

'But I say it's very relevant, Milner wouldn't have had time.'

'There was time for a wave of the hand by either party. That's all he claims. We could have waved to her and she to us.'

'And come back this way to date her up, thirty years later?'

'The Greeks, as usual,' Kenworthy said, 'can help us linguistically.'

'What do you mean?'

'*Nympholepsis.*'

'I'm sorry, I haven't the benefits of an education in Met.'

'A state of euphoria, brought about in pale-faced loiterers by accidentally coming upon a woodland goddess. It happened every other day in the groves of Mount Olympus.'

'Do you think they know that in the Home Office? It'll look good in a "case closed" report, won't it? I rather fancy it. *Nympholepsis. No further action recommended. Signed, D. Stammers, D.C.I.* I must say, it suits dear old Milner, though. *Alone and palely loitering.*'

'*The sedge is withered by the lake,*' Elspeth said.

'You haven't actually met my Chief Constable, have you, Simon?'

'It might help, of course, if you could produce the girl.'

'Oh, yes, where were you at 4.43 on the morning of 23rd April, 1941, and to whom did you wave your hand?'

'She *might* remember,' Kenworthy insisted amicably. 'I mean, God knows why she was sitting half in, half out of her bedroom window at that time of night or day. But if a bomber had come suddenly lumbering out of the trees, not ten feet above her ... well, it would make its mark, wouldn't it? And we *could* perhaps find her. Damn it, I've pulled off longer shots than that in my time. We know who lived in each house, don't we? We can see which houses faced west by south-west. That will narrow things down.'

After some moments, Derek spoke. 'This is going to have its amusing moments, you know. I shall be sent for to supplement this report. *So he waved to her, Stammers, and thirty years later she's come forward to remember waving back at him. Well, not exactly come forward, sir. My brother-in-law suggested ... And you feel that this is conclusive, do you, Stammers?*'

'Is that all that matters to you?' Elspeth asked. 'A credibility rating?'

Neither man directly answered her.

'It isn't exactly conclusive,' Kenworthy said. 'But we'd better have a shot at finding her, anyway. It will help. And I think it might lead us on to other things. I mean, there's more to it than just nympholepsis. Nothing that anybody's going to gaol for, I'll be bound. But if that charmer Menschel had come a couple of minutes later ...'

Stammers suddenly changed down, switched on his nearside flasher, and filtered into a country lane. 'We'll find her,' he said, with no consciousness of melodrama.

CHAPTER SEVEN

For three quarters of a mile they fretted behind a tractor drawing a muddy empty trailer.

'Shot in the dark, this one, Simon. But I've others in the armoury if this fails. I wish we lived a little nearer Wiltshire.'

At last the driver of the tractor put out an arm, pulled up obliquely across the road, and got off his seat to unfasten a gate.

'I don't even know if she's still alive, the woman I'm taking us to see. Except that her existence is too charmed for her ever to die. And not the healthiest of charmers at that. You'll see—perhaps.'

The trailer bumped across the verge into a field, and Stammers raised a finger in friendly acknowledgement. The gesture seemed to confirm that this really was his country.

'Emma Pascoe, the woman we are calling on. If she's still alive, she'll be turned ninety. She left Yarrow Cross, of course, when the rest of them did. No husband, ever, reared a boy of her own, and then three grand-sons, real tearaways, when their parents died. That's how I come to know her so well: the Pascoe kids. Sam, Tom and Darkie. Every crime in the calendar: gas-meters, church poor boxes, breaking into cricket pavilions. Big stuff. Big enough to scare half the county, anyway. And it wasn't just that they knew how to handle themselves. They didn't know when not to. I've known Darkie get himself eighteen months for resisting arrest on a charge that would only have got him six.

'But Emma knew how to deal with them—and me. She's only a little woman, and those three were six-footers, but when she said turn, they turned. I wasn't exactly the apple of her eye when I was a detective-sergeant, but she'd known for years, without ever liking it, which side her bread was buttered.

'"Which of them is it you're after this time?" she'd ask, and I'd tell her. And in my younger days, I'd still take the trouble to explain to her what it was all about. But she hardly ever listened. She wasn't interested. I don't think she believed me. She was a wicked bitch in her own right, but she was also a realist. She played along when tactics demanded it. '"Is it Darkie again?" she'd ask, she always did have a soft spot for Darkie—he was the wildest and dimmest of the bunch.

'"Afraid so, Ma," I'd say, and "I'll tell him when he comes in," she'd croak. "He'll be round. You can depend on it." And I could. While the D.I. was still wondering whether he ought to issue firearms to make this arrest, Darkie would shuffle shame-faced into the station, start emptying his pockets on to the counter before we'd even told him what it was about. She had those three where she wanted them.'

They came into a village, clay and thatch cottages huddled round an unimposing but clinically perfect Norman church tower. Stammers turned into a close of some dozen modern council houses.

'Including four old people's bungalows. It's one of the things this county does rather well. But there was more than the usual brouhaha when Emma Pascoe got an allocation. Some people can't live and let live.'

She came to the door with the match-stick frailty of a body that was carrying on by some scarcely credible fluke. There was a hump between her shoulders that left her head and neck sagging with her face almost parallel to the ground.

But nothing was amiss with Emma Pascoe's wits. She recognised Derek Stammers as if she had been expecting his visit; yet it was, he said, three or four years since she had seen him.

'You can't leave well alone, can you, you people?'

'I'm not bringing trouble, this time.'

'That'll be the day. You'd best come in.'

'It would be as well.'

Elspeth had made to stay in the car, but Derek thought otherwise.

'If I'd a W.P.C. handy, I wouldn't drop in on Emma without a chaperone. But don't try to talk to her.'

The quarters were roomy enough for them not to overcrowd the place—an L-shaped room with cooking and storage angled off from eating and living. Most of the furnishings were poorish, immediate post-war. The Pascoes had not had much to bring out of Yarrow Cross with them. It was odds and ends, rather than major pieces, that pointed to the past: an ornamental clock with only an hour hand, a scene of classical mythology on its glass panel.

'Why can't you let him be? He's only been out a fortnight.'

'Who? Darkie, you mean?'

'Who else? You haven't come to arrest *me*, I hope.' She spoke fluently but damply over toothless gums. If she had dentures, she was not wearing them.

'I haven't come to arrest anyone.'

'He hasn't been out a fortnight,' she repeated. 'And he's been working since Monday.'

'Working where?'

'Catching turkeys.'

'Sounds a bit seasonal,' Kenworthy said.

Derek explained. 'Turkey batteries. Massive scale. Local speciality. They're trying to create a national demand for turkey all the year round. And someone has to catch the birds in the breeding sheds—ready for slaughter. A labourer catches something like a thousand birds a day. Lungful of feathers. And where's Sammy these days, Ma?'

'Still in Essex. *And* going straight.'

'I hope Darkie will, this time.'

Stammers had grown out of the years when a new bout of freedom for Darkie Pascoe would have sent a chit round all divisions.

'How many years of the last twenty has he spent inside, anyway?'

'Sixteen. If you want it in months and days, I've got it written down.'

She moved towards a wad of papers stuffed into an old toast-rack.

Sixteen years: and there wasn't an offence on the sheet that made an atom of sense: breaking in where there was nothing to take, trying to sell hot loot on the open market, hoping to kip down for a fortnight in a suburban semi while the owners were on holiday. There was nothing of the master-planner about Darkie Pascoe. Stammers was anxious to get rid of the subject; but some patience was still necessary.

'Sammy's not been in your hands fifteen years. Tom's still at the garage. So it must be Darkie you're after. Like you had him on suspicion in Wymondham market-place when he hadn't been out a month. You got him a year for that—for standing looking at a fish-stall with his hands in his pockets.'

'*I* didn't. And I've told you: I'm not after anybody. Only information.'

'You want me to put someone else away for you?'

'No. I want your help to get someone off the hook.'

'I'll believe that when I see it.' But her curiosity was stronger than her bitterness. 'Who is it, then?'

'Nobody you know. At least, somebody you might have heard of.'

'What sort of a riddle is that?'

'Ma, I want you to try to cast your mind back to the early days of the war in Yarrow Cross.'

'Oh, aye?'

And Stammers was helped to point the conversation. A vertical take-off jet, from the American base at Lakenheath, no stranger to south-west Norfolk, opened its taps somewhere on the sky-line.

'Much troubled by low flying aircraft, Ma?'

'We get used to them.'

'It was a low flying aircraft I wanted to ask you about, Ma, one particular one, one that you might possibly remember.'

'I know.'

'You know. How do you know? Listen, Ma, I haven't stopped telling you, yet.'

Kenworthy looked at her and wondered whether her faculties were indeed declining. But there was life and intelligence in her eyes, resentful as they were, blazingly angry, now, behind the folds of flaky skin. 'I said, didn't I, you can't let well alone. Darkie had nothing to do with that.'

'I've told you I'm not talking about Darkie.'

'If you want to go digging up those years, why don't you go and ask the Prudhoes? Ask Sally Hammond.'

'Who's Sally Hammond?'

She looked at him as if he were trying to tell her some outrageous lie. 'Well, who else does he come back to see?'

'Who? To see Sally Hammond? You mean Darkie?'

'Darkie? What would Darkie be hanging about her for? I mean the airman. You know I mean the airman.'

'Which airman is that, then?'

She looked as if she might be going to spit. 'You make me sick,' she said. 'How many airmen have you got eating your heart out, then? All the others were killed when they crashed, weren't they? I said to Darkie, "You have nothing to do with it," I said. "It'll bounce back on you".'

Suddenly tears poured out over her cheeks and she began to sob as she talked. She had been talking to them from an aggressive stance on the hearthrug. Now Elspeth helped her to a chair.

'Mr Stammers, don't take Darkie away from me again. He's always been good to me, has Darkie, kinder than either of the other two, though I've seen less of him than I have of them—thanks to you.'

Elspeth helped her to unscrew her handkerchief.

'Mr Stammers, I've always played fair with you. You can't say I haven't. In those early days I had to believe, didn't I, that a short sharp warning couldn't do them any harm. Well, it did stop the other two. But Darkie's had sixteen years behind bolts and bars, Mr Stammers, and now you've come back to something that happened while I was still calling myself a young woman.'

Stammers had no immediate come-back. Kenworthy sympathised. How could Derek ask any more questions without revealing how little they knew? And the moment she saw that, this old woman was going to clam up irretrievably.

She was nothing like as naive as she was trying to make herself seem.

Kenworthy had meant to leave the talking to Stammers. He had honestly intended to stay somnolent in the back seat. Any contribution he might have made would have been a smiling, unobtrusive, side-of-the-mouth suggestion as they drove back along country lanes, well out of hearing of any of the principals.

But he could not resist intrusion now. He was in a position to question from ignorance. It was the essential advantage that Stammers lacked.

'Mrs Pascoe, you must forgive me. I've come new to all this. Down from London, a long way from Yarrow Cross in space and time. Who *is* Sally Hammond?'

She looked at him in visible uncertainty whether to play along with him or not. His blue eyes exuded deeply human understanding. He had the knack of focusing them beyond the person at whom he was looking, which gave an impression of penetration into depth. Nine-tenths of his success, his detractors said, came from his ability to inspire false confidence.

Elspeth waited with silent breath. She knew that the human understanding was real, but she did not doubt his ability to make ruthless tactical use of it. Stammers stayed silent, content to withdraw; he might have his faults, and professional jealousy might have figured amongst them in his time, but it was not to the fore now.

Emma Pascoe returned Kenworthy's gaze, her eyes looking up from their sockets in her effort to hold up her head. For silent seconds they confronted each other in acknowledged challenge.

'You don't know who Sally Hammond is?'

Her tone was difficult to analyse. There was more than an element of derision in it, the conscious superiority of sitting on knowledge that is wanted, however trivial it might be. But there was a certain teasing softness, too, a suggestion that she might be wheedled into talking, in her own time and on her own terms. Emma Pascoe had all the marks of a primitive; her outlook must surely be savagely parochial; now, ending her days in this Rural District old folk's bungalow she was, at twelve miles, probably as far as she had ever been from where she was born. But there was a brute shrewdness in her intelligence, sharpened perhaps by the struggle her brain was having with the wearied flesh.

'Why don't you ask her herself who she is?'

Kenworthy refused to be tempted into the obvious. 'I gather she was the young lady who waved to the airman,' he said inconsequentially.

'Sitting on the window-sill in her nightdress. Sally Carver she was, in those days. She'd have waved to an angel, if he'd dropped from the skies wearing uniform. It was in the Carver blood.'

Her eyes glittered, a plea to be pressed. But Kenworthy also knew how to tease.

'Did you wave to the airman too?' he asked her. And Emma Pascoe laughed, an unexpected mixture of cynicism and pure amusement.

'I waved to a Volunteer, long before the first war. Only he didn't come back looking for me.'

'But the airman came for Sally?'

She could not help being scornful of his ignorance. 'He was too late, wasn't he? And he got into trouble for it—though nothing like the trouble he's in this time.'

Again, Kenworthy chose to leave a major issue unexplored. The surrounding villages knew, of course, about the death of the lance-corporal; but it was interesting, to say the least, that the old woman had pin-pointed Milner.

Kenworthy let it slide; that horse would find its own way home in time, its bridle dangling. He hoped the point would not be lost on Derek. 'He was too late, was he? But he did succeed in contacting her?'

'You'd better ask her.'

'I shall.'

'Well, then.'

They looked at each other, stalemate threatened. But if Kenworthy was prepared to let the dialogue flag, the old woman wasn't.

'I could strike a bargain, Mr Londoner, for what I know about Sally Hammond.'

'Kenworthy's my name. And you couldn't, because I'm not allowed to make bargains. I might be more efficient, in the short run, if they'd let me. But I'm glad they don't. It would complicate life.'

'How complicate it?'

'When I've finished with a case I want to move on to the next without having to remember a new set of rules. And I like people to know where they stand with me, just as they know where they stand with you.'

'They do that,' she said.

Again a short silence. Kenworthy was winning: she was puzzled by him.

'So you'll be off to see Sally Hammond?' she said at last.

'If I can find her.'

'That won't be hard. Anyone can tell you—except *him*.' A scornful dart of the eyes towards Derek. 'Perhaps he's never thought of looking. It takes a Londoner. You'll find she's changed, Mr Kenworthy. She's not Sally Carver any more.'

'No?'

'She's got what she deserved. And I say that, not knowing what might happen to me one day.'

'Enigmatic,' Kenworthy said.

'That's a big word, Mr Kenworthy.'

'It means talking in riddles.'

'I don't have to talk in riddles, Mr Kenworthy.'

'I know you don't.'

Then Kenworthy seemed suddenly to change his mind about the whole issue; he smiled, he relaxed, he appeared to relent on all fronts. 'All right. I'll make no promises. But I will at least ask your price.'

'Leave my Darkie out of it.'

'That would be easier to consider if I knew just where he came into it.'

Emma Pascoe's eyes had been restlessly shifting. Now they looked keenly into his. A truth had dawned on her, and she laughed: a cronish cackle that must have been rooted in poetic satisfaction.

'You just don't know, do you? You just don't.'

'No. I just don't.'

'Well, bloody well find out, then.'

Kenworthy got up and moved towards the door. 'All right, we will. We'll be back. What time did you say Darkie finishes work? Derek, I think you'll be able to deal with him without my help, won't you?'

Emma came over to him and grasped his wrists in fingers that were brittly thin but unexpectedly warm. 'Don't take Darkie away again. He's done nothing this time.'

'Perhaps it would help if you got Darkie to come and see us, then he can tell us just how big a nothing it is.'

'You know it wouldn't help—it wouldn't help Darkie. You might not know, but *he* does. *He* knows that Darkie hasn't the sense to speak up for himself, can't open his mouth without landing himself in trouble. That's how it's been all along. That's how *he* earns his living, tricking men like my Darkie into getting themselves put away for three quarters of their natural life.'

Derek shrugged off the onslaught. 'Darkie's been stupid all his life. And what have you ever done to help him? Have you ever told him that a job wasn't safe to touch? Don't you know how senseless he's always been? Last time I talked to Darkie—and it's a long time ago now, years—I told him: if he had a cast-iron alibi, he'd talk his way out of it.'

'You've always picked on him.'

'I'd say he's always picked on me. Just couldn't keep from under my feet.'

They came away. As he was reversing his car in the village close, Derek sighed. 'I don't think we should be too impressed by Emma Pascoe's innuendoes.'

'Nor should we underestimate them. We know there's a connection between Milner and Darkie. That's progress.'

'But Emma doesn't know what Darkie's up to half the time. There was a time when she wasn't past setting jobs up for the lads—and fencing stuff for them—till she found out the hard way she couldn't trust them.'

'I'd like to see Darkie's record, chapter and verse.'

'You shall.'

Stammers pulled up in a lay-by and asked over the car radio for the sheet to be photostatted and delivered to his home that evening. He also set his sergeant on the trail of Sally Hammond, née Carver.

'Should be a matter of desk routine. And I'm grateful for your help, Simon. If time hangs heavy on your hands tomorrow, you're welcome to chat up anyone you like. Lack of official standing might even be an advantage.'

'Distinctly.'

'There's one thing I don't like.' Elspeth spoke from the back of the car.

'What's that, then?'

'Edward Milner talked about being knocked about, on one of his previous encounters. I didn't think we went in for that kind of thing.'

'We don't, not in my department, we don't. I was nothing in those days; a mere nothing. I don't know who authorised that—well, *authorised* is the wrong word.'

'Blind eye to the telescope,' Kenworthy said.

'And, as Milner told you, it was the opposite of helpful.'

'That man!' It might have been Milner who was Elspeth's brother. 'The last man on earth to whom you or anybody else should have shown violence.'

'I've already said, I didn't.'

'And you didn't kick up a fuss about it, either.'

Kenworthy felt obliged to bring in a more whimsical note. '*The last man on earth*—how often has he been the villain in your book, Derek?'

'Seldom. Story-book stuff. Come back to the man you first thought of. That's nearer my experience.'

'And mine. But there have been exceptions.'

'There's one thing I would ask you.' Stammers looked over his shoulder to take in Elspeth as well as Simon. Don't talk to Diana about this. Case-work bores her. And frightens her too, sometimes.'

It was not until they were in their bedroom, getting ready for the evening meal, that Elspeth added her own postscript to this. 'And he wouldn't care for her to think that he was indebted to you for ideas or suggestions. I mean, not that Derek would mind. But I imagine that dear Di gets a bit repetitive at times. Is Derek a good policeman, Simon?'

'A very good policeman indeed, I'd say.'

'You're not just being charitable?'

'I don't think so. We're different, he and I. But if you set me down in his corner of the plain, I doubt whether I'd have got as far up the mountain as he has. In my world, there's more than one route up the scree. Derek's had to make it up the only track that was open to him. That means he must be damned good.'

'But he's lacking something, isn't he? What is it, Simon? Imagination? And yet I've known him all these years, in so far as you can be said to know anyone, even your baby brother—three whole years between us! And I'd not have said that his imagination ...'

'Time!' Kenworthy said. 'That's what he lacks. I mean, it seems to me that he's trying to administer a department and still apply himself to all the detail. That doesn't work these days, even in these wilds.'

'It doesn't leave him time for Diana, does it?'

'Time to love her, you mean? I don't mean make love to her.'

'He used to idolise her.'

'It's like Cain and Abel, Elspeth. She doesn't care for the smoke from his particular sacrifice.'

Kenworthy went up to his wife and put his hands on the cool flesh above her elbows. She was standing in her slip, her frock for the evening laid out on the bed.

'We're lucky, you and I. And yet, on balance, we've had less time together than the Stammers.'

'It isn't a question of luck. It's a question of attitude, whether one's together or apart. I'm worried for Derek and Diana, though.'

'Perhaps because you're trying to look at them through what you take to be Derek's eyes.'

'On the contrary, I'm trying to see them from Diana's point of view.'

'Unsafe.'

'Like all attempts at detection.'

He slid his arms down to her waist; but there came a gentle tap of knuckles at the door. They parted as startled as adolescents caught in an illicit moment. And then they both laughed.

Derek was holding a type-written sheet round the door. 'This has just come in. Thought you might like to see ...'

'Well, do come in, Derek, we *are* decent.'

It was the summary of Darkie's record.

B. 1912. Store-breaking 1923, first offender, bound over; 1924 – stealing by finding – shop-breaking – 1925, birched – 1926, 27, 28. Borstal, 1929.

'And we've had no difficulty finding Sally Hammond. She's paraplegic. Whip-lash injury in a car accident, four years ago. She's been in a Home Counties hospital ever since. Little hope of improvement. I suppose that's what Emma Pascoe means by getting what she deserved.'

'How horrible can you get?'

Kenworthy glanced again at Darkie's history.

Royal Norfolk Regiment, 1941 – A.W.O.L. Various Glasshouses: Colchester, Sowerby Bridge, Aldershot. 1943, theft of W.D. property, viz one leather jerkin. Holland, 1944, looting. Discharged, 1947. Breaking and entering, 1948, eighteen months. 1950 four years for resisting arrest and grievous bodily harm – broke policeman's arm with the leg of a chair.

'Hardly a bird of Milner's feather,' Kenworthy said. And he remembered, ironically, old Emma Pascoe's plea.

He's always been good to me, has Darkie—kinder than the other two.

'Don't let it spoil your appetite,' Stammers said. 'There are certain aromas rising from the kitchen. I fancy Diana has excelled herself.'

Seven years, 1953. Seven years, 1959. Suspected person charge, 1965.

'That's the one that got under Emma Pascoe's skin.'

But who was to blame Stammers and his minions if they'd been a bit ferocious? Life, limb and property on the Norfolk-Suffolk border were safer, by and large, when Darkie Pascoe was away. That was a state of affairs that Derek was paid his salary to maintain.

Pascoe's last sentence had been a ten-year stretch in 1967. He seemed to have got himself a chore in the wake of some managerial mob—fall guy, obviously. They'd done a wages snatch and left him behind, stunned by a security guard's club. So, with normal remission, he'd just come out. To catch turkeys.

'Drinks in five minutes,' Derek said, beginning to slide out of the room.

'I'll tell you what. I'd like a note of all Milner's dates.'

'After supper, surely. But first things first, Simon.'

Carbonnades à la Flamande. Diana certainly knew what she was about. And a dry Burgundy. Derek had irritating trouble, trying to open the bottle with an instrument too twee and flimsy for the job. He had to filter out bits of cork through a coffee-strainer, which exasperated Di.

But she behaved very well at table; even managed a certain charm as if it were not costing her an effort. (Though, Kenworthy thought to himself, no one would ever recognise how much of the required effort was actually being put in by Elspeth.)

After the meal, they polished off the washing up by communal effort. Then they settled down to play *Scrabble*, it having come out in small talk that both couples sometimes indulged. But here the fragility of Diana's self-discipline began to show through again. There were family interpretations of the rules; and though each side was eager to defer to the other, Diana's mistrust was a little too transparent: especially in the matter of two-letter words. Even when faced with the authority of the dictionary, she was reluctant to believe in *io* as a cry of jubilation.

Derek was called to the phone just as Elspeth was on tenterhooks with a seven-letter word and its fifty-point bonus. The receiver was in the hall, and they could hear no more than a word or two of Derek's voice. In fact, all three of them were doing their best to appear not to be listening. But they heard him put the instrument down and dial afresh; and then the same yet again.

A stronger woman than Diana might have rolled her eyes in comic abandon; but Diana drew her bottom lip inwards over her teeth. Derek came back, but only partly round the door.

'Like to get your hat and coat, Simon? Sorry, ladies.'

Diana flicked her rack of letters away from her, a good deal more violently than she had intended, so that they flew along the polished table-top and spilled on the floor. Elspeth went on her hands and knees to help to pick them up.

'Menschel. Milner's given them the slip. My bloke, too. And the old quack's certain that he'll make for you-know-where. I've just rung the army. They've nothing on for the next hour or two.'

Kenworthy joined his brother-in-law at the hall-stand.

'Are you going to be out all night?' Diana called.

'We'll be out till we've finished.'

Elspeth came out and planted a kiss on Simon's eye-brow. 'Take care, darling.'

'I hardly think that Milner will attack us.'

CHAPTER EIGHT

There had been a little more rain this evening, but it was fine again now. The light from the headlamps was reflected from the puddles in a strange manner, a flimsy, transient luminescence that seemed to climb the tree trunks as their tyres hissed on the wet roads.

'One thing puzzles me a little, Derek, I'd have been tempted to give Milner his head years ago, let him loose in there to see what would have happened.'

'I wanted to. But I was working for a man in those days who had a marked dislike for fantasy of any kind. And the chance was only a fleeting one. Sometimes the range isn't in use for weeks on end, but that hardly ever happened when Milner was in the offing.'

'Which reminds me, Milner's dates.'

Derek slid his hand in the cubby-hole and passed over a note-book. 'You'll find them somewhere in the last few pages.'

Kenworthy studied the notes with the help of a torch. 'As I thought. Whenever he came here, Darkie was temporarily at liberty.'

'Blast! I never thought of that.'

'Why should you? If we hadn't called on grandma this afternoon, we'd never have thought of Darkie.'

There was another kind of reflection, even more transitory than the tenuous light from the puddles. The Forestry Commission had fixed little mirrors on stakes at intervals to try to scare the deer back from the road.

'So it's still nympholepsis, Simon? A night visit, after all that's happened to him?'

'There's more to it. But I still say that's where it started: an image on Milner's consciousness, persisting through concussion and delirium: a picture in the jaws of death. A girl at a window—and something else.'

'What else?'

'That, I hope, we're on the brink of finding out. I think he saw something else that night. If Sally Carver was sitting half in, half out of her bedroom window, it wasn't because she was waiting for the arrival of an aircraft that she couldn't have known about. She may, of course, have been merely sleepless. She may be a poetically dreamy type. But it's also possible that she might have been looking at something, or for something, that had awakened her. Something that Edward Milner saw, too.'

'Something related to the nightly comings and goings of Darkie Pascoe?'

'I daren't take it as far as that yet.'

'Darkie was very active at this particular period, as he was at any time when not actually behind bars. And I'm not pretending that we know all his transgressions.'

'But let's not take it too fast, Derek. There are terrible dangers in exercising the imagination. One's too apt to find an attractive branch halfway up that takes one's mind off the rest of the tree. I say its conceivable, but I still have to be convinced, that Milner saw something in Yarrow Cross that was branded into his brain as indelibly and as tantalisingly as the girl in the window. But we mustn't blind ourselves. He might possibly have discovered something else when he came back to try to find the girl.

'When Milner came back after the war he'd expect, as would any other rational being, that this area had been given back to its original occupants. He might even have trespassed unwittingly the first time. In any case, he'd come a long way and probably hadn't much time. He sees no one about, he says "Oh! Bugger it!" and goes in for a look round. And what's his next move?'

'Straight into the local mush.'

'Refusing to talk. Refusing to say what his obvious next step would be—to do what you and I did: get hold of the six-inch map, the electoral roll, contact someone else who'd lived there. How long would he beat about that bush before coming across one or other of the Pascoes? The only thing that worries me is that the Pascoes aren't his company.'

'Darkie Pascoe is the complete, the utter, the irrational recidivist. Intelligence, common sense don't enter into it. He's never learned fear of reprisals; he never even knows when the game is up. I've taken loot out of poacher's pockets sewn in the inside of Darkie's jacket, so weighed down he could hardly walk or breathe, and he's expressed surprise that the stuff was there. No. Darkie wouldn't impress Milner.'

'So they must have a peculiar common cause.'

'Perhaps.'

And Kenworthy quoted the old woman. *'I said to Darkie, you have nothing to do with it, I said. It'll bounce back on you.'*

'We shall know in a little while, perhaps. I'd not be happy trying to rest a case on a quote from Emma Pascoe.'

'We're not resting a case yet, are we? We're still trying to feel our way into one.'

Derek turned into the same lane, scarcely more than a broadened forest ride, that they had used the previous day. They were checked at the barrier by a pair of military policemen, who were clearly expecting them, and conducted to the duty office, where a captain in field service gear was reading Dick Francis at a bare metal desk, roasting parts of his body at a tinny old electric fire.

'The O.C's told me to tell you that you've got till precisely four a.m. As luck has it, we've got a new intake this evening. They're just squaring their gear up and we propose to baptise them at dawn stand-to. Till then, it's all yours. Want some of us to come with you?'

'No, thank you. The fewer the quieter. I'm expecting some of my own chaps as reserves, but I want them strictly in the background. When they arrive, if you'd be so kind as to keep them in camp unless I call them forward by radio. This is one trespasser that I want to encourage, up to a point. That is, providing it's safe under foot.'

'How far do you propose to penetrate?'

'Just to the village.'

'That's safe enough. We like to keep the general public scared, but we're pretty careful. Our resident sappers go over the terrain after every exercise. The bit that interests you was reported clear this afternoon. Nothing lying about.'

'Is it safe to take the car?'

'I wouldn't. Strictly for feet or track-layers.' The captain looked down at their genteel shoes. 'We can lend you rubber boots.'

And when that transaction was complete—it involved a surprised but obliging storeman, whose headquarters was the spiritual home of a brag school—they set out through the scrub.

At first they tried to walk carefully, the weeds and grasses swishing about their ankles, their heels and insteps chafing inside the ill-fitting gum-boots. Sound travelled over great distances; and it might not take more than one realistic scare to make Milner change his mind. But after some minutes of slow and heavy plodding, they decided to throw immediate discretion to the winds. No amount of effort was going to produce perfect silence, and it was better perhaps to press on regardless and get the essential movement over. Once they got amongst the wrecked buildings, they could enjoy as much peace and quiet as they wanted.

So they pushed at last through the undergrowth into the heart of the old village: the old Cattle Feed hoarding, illegible in incipient moonlight, the hulk of rubble into which the lance-corporal had fired; hard to distinguish from half a dozen like it.

They paused to get their bearings. Both men now knew the ground plan of the original Yarrow Cross pretty well by heart: the post office, the church, the inn, the vicarage. Some cottages, particularly those built from clay-lump in the local tradition, had suffered more than others, adding misshapen debris to the confusion. And everywhere not merely gorse, cow parsley and hog-weed had grown, but thickets of self-sown saplings, making nonsense of any attempt to be certain of the line of alleys, streets and pavements. Against a barn wall the old yellow disc of an A.A. place-sign was chipped and rusted: a natural target for any man with a surplus round to loose off; and it was difficult to believe that this, then, must have been an outside wall, a landmark for traffic that had come in about its lawful business from the main road.

They looked again at the low bank where the N.C.O. had died.

And, yes, they knew it already, but now they could see it: the house in which Milner had been spotted could indeed have been the one from which the girl had waved. Its front windows, all that was left of them, faced almost due west. A bomber lumbering and bucketing home from the Ruhr could have come skimming over this roof from behind. Milner could indeed have looked down on her.

Nympholepsis?

Kenworthy looked over towards the church tower. Seventeen minutes to five the hands had marked, so Milner said, as indestructible in his memory as the girl herself. And that could probably be checked against somebody's archives. They had narrowly missed the tower, he said. It was about a hundred and fifty yards from the house. Well: that fitted in with the line of flight.

So for how long, in seconds, had Milner had this corner of the village in his field of vision? Kenworthy tried to do a rough mental calculation but knew it was a waste of time, because the speed of the plane was guesswork. Between five and ten seconds? Nearer five than ten?

What could Milner have observed in five seconds—with a deduction for delay in his reactions? Disturbed as he must have been by his sudden sight of the gap in the trees?

Disturbed? Or put on his mettle, perhaps? Suddenly more perceptive than he'd ever been in his life before? Perhaps

Menschel would know the answer to that one.

Wasn't it nearer the mark to think of it as one-tenth vision and nine-tenths prolonged hallucination?

And what sort of basis for inference was that?

What was the use of all this feverish speculation anyway? How could they even begin to guess at what he might have seen? They would need to see Yarrow Cross as Milner had first seen it, from the right angle, in precisely the right light of dawn, with precisely the right strands of mist.

Kenworthy had the weird feeling that Yarrow Cross lay all about him; that it could tell them everything—and would tell them nothing. That any attempt at reconstruction was a waste of time. That it would be far easier to get Milner to tell them, better still, to sit quietly hidden whilst he showed them.

'How long do you reckon it will take him to get here?'

'Don't know,' Derek said. 'Depends on what lifts he gets, how far he has to cover on foot.'

'If he's hoping for a lift on this last stretch, he'll be a long time. We didn't pass a car. How long has he been on the road?'

'First missed at 8.10.'

'He'll be lucky to get here by four. It would be just like him to come blundering through the dawn barrage.'

'On the other hand, he could be here any minute.'

'I hope not, because I want to have another quick look at the surrounds. After that, I suggest we retire to close cover and just wait.'

They passed the light of their torches over the interior of the Carvers' cottage. But it told them nothing. It couldn't tell them anything. Nothing had changed since their visit yesterday morning. How could anything have changed? Rubble, plaster, rotting laths, and a sudden scurrying where some rodent was scavenging amongst the rubbish.

Outside the cottage, along its northern wall, there was a comparatively clear space—comparatively clear, that is, of solid debris, or the visible lines of any wall. But they had not penetrated far through its particularly wiry tangle of weeds before they came upon a small area of broken and uneven flag-stones that had once obviously been someone's yard.

And in the same movement each man laid his hand on the other's cuff.

'Steady, Derek!'

'Watch it, Simon!'

Lying in front of them, standing out starkly in its shadow under their torch-light, on a patch of stone that had been cleared as if to display a museum exhibit, there lay the small pineapple outline of a hand grenade, the old Mills 36, that had served the infantry in two world wars.

'And they told us the place was cleared this afternoon.'

'Do you know much about these things, Derek?'

'Enough to leave them alone.'

'I remember them from my rookie days. I suppose it was thrown from the prairie out there, and hasn't gone off.'

The ring and the split pin were missing. So was the clip-handle that they held down. The notched end of the plunger, a little silver glint, protruded from the upper end of the bomb.

'I remember that happened once when I was under training. Either the spring's broken, or there's some obstruction in the sleeve—a bit of mud or grit that's prevented detonation. When it happened to us, an old sweat sergeant with brass buttons on his service-dress had to get down behind sandbags and pot at it with a rifle. He got it first time, but I never heard language like his in my life.'

'Nobody's going to fire at it where that lies. Where could he get a sight from? This is going to give the demolition boys a right old head-ache.'

'They'll have to be told before that lot comes swarming over at stand-to.'

Kenworthy crouched on his hands and knees and took a very close look.

'Not getting any sudden new ideas, I hope, Simon?'

'Just wondering.'

'Well, let's go and do our wondering a hundred and fifty yards away.'

'No need for that. Sixty yards is about the normal lethal range, if I remember it. I'm just marvelling how a little thing like that could bugger up our night out.'

'It'll bugger up Milner's, if he steps on it without seeing it.'

'I doubt it.'

'How do you mean, you doubt it?'

Kenworthy did not answer, but walked some yards away, to the nearest standing fragment of wall, and looked down over it.

'You're not thinking of anything, Simon?'

'You go and sit it out in Sally Carver's living-room, Derek.'

'Like hell! And let you ...'

'I've just been looking for somewhere to throw it.'

'It'll go off in your hand if you touch it.'

'It won't. It can't. If I can pick it up by the notch in the plunger, it won't go off till I tell it to—perhaps not even then. If the plunger slips, it'll either stick again, as it has now, or it will percuss a little rim-fire cartridge. That sets fire to a four-second fuse. And four seconds is a hell of a long time, Derek. It's all the P.B.I. had in action. And this is probably a training model anyway, which would have seven seconds. That's an eternity. They didn't use seven second fuses in battle, because they gave the recipient time to lob the bloody thing back.'

'I'll not be a party to it, Simon. Anyway, look!'

He dived and came up with something in his hand.

'The clip. So the split pin must be somewhere in the offing. So it obviously wasn't thrown here from the prairie. The pin was pulled out here, on this spot.'

'Which a bloke wouldn't do unless he knew for certain that the thing *wasn't* going to go off. Give that to me, Derek.'

Stammers handed him the curved strip of metal, and in one swoop Kenworthy had the grenade in his hand with the clip back in position and the plunger secure. He began to try to shift the stubborn base-plug.

'Simon! That's enough, now.'

'It's not enough. We can't leave it like this.'

The plug suddenly yielded to the ball of his thumb.

'As I thought. No detonator. No spring even. No wonder the plunger was loose and—well! damn me! That's the first time I've ever seen one with the filler-screw missing. Derek, this one's been emptied. No basic charge, even. This is somebody's souvenir—an empty case. What a very gentlemanly gesture on somebody's part. But how discouraging it could have been. Darkie Pascoe's work, do you think?'

'Darkie's definitely not that kind of gentleman. He'd never have thought of this in ten thousand years. He couldn't see two moves ahead in any game—even one to save his own skin!'

'Let's move back into the shadows, then.' Kenworthy slipped the bomb into his rain-coat pocket. 'No need to go boasting to Elspeth about this. She wouldn't strike me any medal. She wouldn't understand.'

They moved out to a sheltered point some thirty yards outside the village.

'One thing, Derek, we now know we're not wasting our time. Somebody else is expecting Milner tonight, somebody who wanted to warn him off, without wishing him any harm.'

'Could be. Sometime soon, we've got to get in here by arrangement and start digging in and round that spot.'

'Digging!' Kenworthy's enthusiasm was sudden and explosive. 'That's it, Derek—digging!'

'That's what I said, isn't it? We'll get the lads out with picks and shovels the moment we can clear it with the army.'

'That's not what I mean. I mean: what Milner saw. A man, two men, a group of men, digging. Looking out of his turret: framed in the same proscenium as the girl at the window: somebody digging. The clank of shovels: that's what woke the girl: something she heard but couldn't see, because it was alongside the north wall of the house, where there aren't any windows.'

'Hidden treasure?' Derek was sceptical, but his sarcasm was playful.

'Something they were putting away? Something they were retrieving? Loot? Secrets? A corpse? Something they wanted stashed away for the duration? The night this happened, had they already had notice to quit? That's something you can check, Derek, if you can't quote it off the cuff. A girl at a window and men digging: something etched into Milner's retina like a snap from a Polaroid Swinger.'

Kenworthy was almost breathless in his eagerness. But Derek was too orthodox and cautious to allow himself to be infected. 'You do push things from simple beginnings, Simon.'

'Of course.'

'You were talking not so long ago about the dangers of imagination. Isn't the worst of those the illusion of certainty?'

'Maybe. But it's an illusion worth having a butcher's at while you're about it.'

'Is this how you've cracked all the big ones, Simon?'

'Pursuing fantasies until there was not a trickle of life's blood left in them. And developing a thick skin for the moment that they fizzle out. When that happens, you just move on to the next, and do the same with that.'

'Well, I've no doubt that in the last ten seconds you've taken this one several stages further. Are you ready to reject it yet?'

'Far from it. I see men digging. Three men. The Pascoe brothers. Something their grandma knew about. Something even she didn't trust. That's why she warned Darkie off, when Milner came round asking questions.'

'You make things fit, Simon.'

'That's the moment when I do begin to scent danger, when those about me start agreeing with me.'

'You must lead your sergeants a hell of a dance.'

'Just now and then I've suspected one or the other of them of rather enjoying it.'

Over at the camp a bugler sounded *Last Post*. It was almost half a mile away, but the sound travelled clearly on the moist air. They heard the crunch of his heels as he marched back to the guard-room.

Kenworthy went and urinated against a relic of crumbling, overgrown wall. 'And now I suggest we pipe down. Milner's an ex-serviceman, and if he's near enough to have heard that bugle, he'll not move in until he hears *Lights Out*.'

Derek moved some distance away and took cover behind a low coping.

And whatever the years of mock battle had done to the village, it had not cleared it of wild life. There were still creatures that seemed to have accommodated themselves to the intermittent racket. An owl flew over them, huge wings that dipped only once or twice, without a sound. Nearer at hand Kenworthy heard some much smaller animal: a field-mouse, perhaps, climbing about blades of grass with as much confidence as if they were tubular scaffolding.

Was your journey really necessary?

Did men, too, climb obstacles that they could just as easily go round?

He heard the movement stop. Feeding, perhaps. Nibbling at something. Preening its whiskers.

The last call of the day came from the camp square, the bottom G deep throated and pure. They weren't near enough, there were too many trees in the way, to see the lights in the huts go out one by one. But Kenworthy could picture it. He spent half his life picturing things he couldn't see. Sometimes he was wrong. Often.

Men digging. The Pascoe brothers.

The stars were unaffected by military routines. They were cold, with a stereoscopic impression of depth. Sometimes you were aware of it, sometimes not. Tonight Kenworthy was. It was going to be a cold night; a frost perhaps. Poor sods at first light; cold rifle-butts.

Retrieving something? Stashing something away?

There were other sounds in the over-lapping folds of the

night: a dog baying, out on a farm beyond the preserves of the M of D; a cow lowing; a car on a distant high-road, free of radar traps along the dead straight, blowing the guts out of the engine. Nearer, much nearer, a moped, pushed to its last resource at full throttle. People must be anxious to get home tonight; or else to get away. Headlamps played optical tricks through the pine trunks.

And then the first sound that didn't belong to the dereliction that was Yarrow Cross. If there were ghosts in the old village, then they preferred the form of furry little animals and dry-winged, blundering moths. But this new sound was no ghost, either. Kenworthy had done his share of night-watching. He knew a human footfall when he heard one, even if it came singly.

And this one wasn't coming singly. Its perpetrator was making no more noise than he could help, but he was no born scout. Over towards where an arc of older trees crowded in on the village, towards the eastern edge, Kenworthy heard a man coming through grass. He heard a foot stubbed against a stone. He heard the man stop several times to listen.

Had Derek heard? Had Derek allowed himself to doze off?

Kenworthy pushed himself up on his elbows and peered. Looking for what? The indiscreet flash of a torch? A shadow that shouldn't have moved?

A twig snapped; or perhaps it didn't. A stone fell from a loose coping; but that must always be happening, out here, without immediate human agency. A jig-saw of sound, normal and abnormal; Kenworthy struggled to make sense, movement, purpose out of it, knew that he was failing. They must wait.

Then a hare got up, started from fairly close to where Kenworthy thought he had placed the newcomer, came dashing diagonally across the middle distance like a train up a cutting, shot close to where Kenworthy and Stammers were lying, caught their scent and changed its line of flight at an abrupt angle.

Milner, if Milner it was, must be standing still, wondering if the animal had given him away. For half a minute there was no sound of his progress. Some other animal—the field-mouse of some minutes ago?—ran over Kenworthy's foot.

And then there was a scuffle. Milner had arrived on the stage; and clearly he was not alone. Perhaps his companion had come with him; perhaps he had come earlier and quietly waited for him; perhaps they had arrived simultaneously from different quarters.

It would come to matter, how they had arrived; but it did not matter now. What did matter was that Milner and his companion apparently no longer thought it necessary to conceal their progress. There was a scuffle: limbs thrashing through the herbiage. A body thumped down on the hard earth, picked himself up again. There were repeated crumps of fists against flesh and bone, the groans and grunts of men putting desperate weight behind their punches.

One thing was predictable: they were too concentrated on their own problems to be on the look-out for strangers. Kenworthy got to his feet and began to run towards them. Derek read his mind and was no more than a yard and a half behind him.

When they were within about fifty yards of their objective, one of the men screamed: a horrifying shriek, the howl of a man, as they were to know within less than a minute, who knew that this was death.

Kenworthy broke into a sprint, cursing the rubber boots, swinging round to his left so that he could come in from a flank. Derek needed no telling to wheel in from the other direction, so that they came down on the stone-flagged yard like the jaws of a pair of calipers.

One man down on his knee was bending over another, his hat pushed to the back of his head. They knew that stylish felt: it was part and parcel of Edward Milner.

'I'm trying to turn him over. He's been knifed. I'm trying to get it out of him, but I'm not sure it's the proper thing. Will it increase the bleeding?'

The blood smelt so sickly, you could taste it. Milner was kneeling in it, his suit soaked, he did not seem to know. Kenworthy's hands were tacky with it, he never did recall how he had plunged them into it.

They got the body on to its belly.

'Never mind, Milner. It makes no difference to him whether you pull it out or leave it where it is. He couldn't care less.'

Derek shone the full flush of his torch down on a middle-aged, badly shaved, grime-lined and terrified face.

'Darkie Pascoe,' he told Kenworthy.

CHAPTER NINE

She sat up in bed, a loose bed-jacket over a translucent night-dress in turquoise nylon; for ever destined, it seemed, to make her crashing first appearances in this sort of attire.

A hospital in the Home Counties. Past her mid-forties, now, but there was something about that face. That first impact stuck in Kenworthy's brain as the earlier one had in Milner's. Vitality; a readiness to burst into laughter; an ebullient enjoyment of the absurd; a picture, ironically, of bounding health.

'You'll find her,' the Sister had said. 'Near the middle on the left. You can't miss her. She radiates through that ward.'

'And if I'm not mistaken, that's just about as far from her actual medical condition ...'

'We get cases like it. Mercifully. It's as if there's some sort of compensation. But she wasn't always like this. When she first came in here ...'

'About four years ago?'

'That's right. For her first year, we couldn't get her to try.'

'You've done well with her.'

'Not me. However, by all means go and talk to her, only don't go worrying her.'

'I told you, this is a social call.'

The Sister seemed on the brink of second thoughts. 'You're sure, Mr Kenworthy?'

'Absolutely. I'm on holiday.'

'A busman's or a Chief Superintendent's?'

'She interests me. But it's only a story I'm trying to round off, Sister, not a case.'

'There's a difference, is there?'

'In your walk of life, too, I would imagine. Don't you ever get fascinated by someone who's not a patient?'

'Yes. But I'm not a policeman.'

As far as Kenworthy was concerned, he was telling the truth. He was out of the case-work. Derek had brow-beaten Milner in the small hours—as near *flagrante delicto*, he pointed out, as two top coppers had ever surprised a man. It wasn't a question of finger-prints: he was still holding the knife.

Milner had strenuously protested his innocence. He had planned a rendezvous with the man they all knew as Darkie Pascoe. Indeed, he was to meet him on the precise spot of the murder and at almost the operative minute.

How had he come to make such an appointment?

There was a public telephone in the central concourse of the hospital.

But he'd have to have an intermediary? Darkie Pascoe wasn't on the phone.

Yes. He'd had an intermediary. But his name wouldn't help, Milner insisted. Relays of detective-sergeants were going to hammer at that for hours.

Milner had come upon Darkie Pascoe struggling with an unknown assailant. No, it was impossible to offer any description. How could one describe a writhing shadow, wrestling by star-light? Especially when you didn't know by star-light which was attacking and which attacked?

And Milner was equally obstinate about his reasons for

yet another visit. He had told Dr Menschel; he had told Dr Menschel everything; and that was confidential. Dr Menschel had agreed, it couldn't help anybody. It couldn't get Milner off this hook; it couldn't affect the case in any way; it could only bring untold misery to people who deserved something better. Something that was of no possible interest to the police.

Just for once in his career, Derek Stammers began wishing that the man would ask for a solicitor: anyone who might possibly try to talk some sense into him.

Kenworthy went back alone to the murder spot whilst the rest of the posse were moving towards the cars. As well as he could, by torch-light and by shuffling his feet, he searched a fifty yard radius for the sheath in which the knife must have been carried. He did not find it. And sitting in Derek's passenger-seat, he insisted, all the way back to headquarters, on its importance.

It was just the sort of weapon, with a vicious curving blade, that had got itself outlawed during the Mods and Rockers spell.

'He didn't have it with him when we picked him up yesterday. He certainly didn't take it with him into the Mental Hospital. And he's hardly likely to have acquired it while he was in there. And he couldn't conceivably have carried it cross-country without a sheath.'

'So he flung the sheath behind his back when he drew the blade: further afield than you were able to look. A thing like that might fly a long way, jettisoned in a moment of savage abandon. We'll find it by daylight.'

'Ministry of Defence permitting.'

'They'll have to bloody well permit this time. If they won't for us, we've still got MI5 making snide noises.'

'True, but if I were you ...' Kenworthy hesitated. He didn't want to talk paternalistically to Derek. He would rather withhold advice altogether. But this did matter.

And Derek looked up with an open face. Elspeth's kid brother.

'If you don't find that sheath, Derek, you've got to think again.'

'I fancy the D.P.P. will be happy enough without it.'

'Oh, blast the D.P.P. So might a jury be. But will you?'

Derek was non-committal, and Kenworthy did not blame him for that. For the next hour or so he had a lot to think about.

Next morning, at breakfast, Derek worn out was just finishing his, and Diana was laying places for Simon and Elspeth, Derek smiled good naturedly.

'Just taken a phone call. We have the sheath. Picked up by the subaltern who led the dawn raid.'

'Congratulations. Sorry I pressed it.'

'Sorry I can't keep you company today.'

'Understood. Elspeth and I thought of looking up Sally Hammond, nevertheless.'

'Why not? No one can stop you sick-visiting on your annual leave. She's only of peripheral interest, anyway.'

'Think so? As far as I'm concerned, it's pure romantic interest.'

'Go to it, then.'

And Sally Hammond was as warm in her welcome of strangers as she would have been of old friends. Sitting up spry amidst a veritable armchair of pillows, they came upon her in the act of lobbing a boiled sweet across the ward. It missed the bed of the patient for whom it was intended, and slid away on the highly polished floor.

'Go and get it for her, will you, Emily? And you'd better give another one to Claire, since she so nearly received that one.'

'Distinguished company for you, Sally.'

'Oh, yes?'

Her bed was a litter of immobilised activity: a badly folded newspaper, a couple of letters, out of their envelopes, a square of handbag mirror, the strewn contents of a make-up compact. She must be Matron's despair: or perhaps that was the sort of hospital this was.

'Strictly off duty, he assures me.'

'You disappoint me, Superintendent. I was hoping I was going to hit the headlines.'

She looked at Kenworthy and Elspeth with a sort of capricious impudence. And Kenworthy wondered: last night's murder had not made the morning's headlines. It was only likely to be reported on regional radio. Here they were not on the East Anglian net. Yet she was not surprised by their visit.

'I remember reading about that case of yours in Norfolk. The one in the marshes. It was better than the Archers.'

'Glad you think so.'

'But I'm sorry you haven't come striding in with your note-book at the ready. *Bed-ridden Sally provides vital clue. Hammond woman to the rescue.*'

'Well, of course, if you like, we'll see what we can do.'

She looked round the ward. 'I know enough about this lot to get them all put away.'

Patients sick with concern for themselves; others already institutionalised and indifferent; a nursing auxiliary helping a bed-case with a crossword anagram; a wheel-chair conference round the corner of a table. The ward had a palpable ambience about it: desperate cases cajoled into living for the minute. And Sally Hammond doing much of the cajoling.

'Nurse Jackson over there, for example, she lets her boyfriend in by the wicket-gate in Sadler Street when she's on nights. I'm sure that comes under the Excessive Liberty of the Subject Act.'

'We would need an unbiased witness.'

'And we strongly suspect that Sue Burden pocketed the ward stakes on the 3.30 at Haydock Park last Thursday.'

'I went down on that one, too.'

Two porters came for a patient with a theatre trolley. There were waves and quips of encouragement from both rows of beds.

'Seriously, though, I suppose you want a statement. *Any-*

thing you say will be taken down in writing, altered and used in evidence against you.'

'That's how I always put it.'

'I mean, I'm the corner-stone of the whole case, aren't I?'

'I'm sure you hold the keys to many a case that's been troubling us for years.'

She leaned back her head against the pillows and closed her eyes, as if become freshly aware of some pain or discomfort that was never ending.

'Enough is enough, Chief Superintendent. I have to go to Physio at half-past. Do you think we can get the business side over by then?'

'We're not here on business, honestly.'

'No? Edward told me I could be expecting you.'

She picked up one of the letters that was lying in front of her, unfolded the sheets, it ran to five double pages. Kenworthy noticed that she only really used her left hand, the other served only for steadying and weight-making.

'And what's this you're doing to him? I must say, my heart was in my mouth when I saw a Norfolk postmark on the envelope. You haven't really had him put away, have you?'

She read aloud Milner's opening lines.

'Dearest Sally. Don't be alarmed when you read this address. I'm not really immolated in a Mental Hospital. They're just letting me use the place as a hotel, to quote their own phrase. I hope to be rallying round the old bedside at the weekend as usual, and I'll tell you the whole story then.'

'And he goes on to say that you'll want confirmation from me—'

'His visits to Yarrow Cross don't seem to work out well for him, do they?'

She did not answer the point, but sat looking at Kenworthy through half screwed-up eyes: assessing, worried, inconclusive. Then suddenly she broke out into a sort of laughter. It was no longer the ebullience of her previous banter. She was trying to be frivolous but it was bitterness that prevailed.

'All right. I'm the girl who waved. A precious three seconds, enough to dominate the lives of how many people? I waved to a passing rear-gunner. I wasn't trying to thumb a lift, or anything like that. I wasn't hoping that he'd jump out of his turret and open his parachute and flutter daintily down into my bed. We just happened to be two people in touch tangentially because we both happened to be awake and looking at each other at an unlikely hour on an evocative May morning.'

Soon, very soon, she was going to know that he was being charged with murder. It wasn't fair to keep it from her a second longer than was necessary.

'I've got to be honest with you, Mrs Hammond.'

'I'll bet our prison cells are full of men who'd say that's the most sinister phrase in your repertoire.'

'I was merely going to say, and it *is* honest, that we know next to nothing about either you or Edward Milner.'

'We are nothing, Mr Kenworthy. As Shelley said, *a mere stain against the white radiance of eternity.*'

'And star-crossed?'

Sally Hammond pouted, finding some semblance to her earlier aplomb.

'I don't know, and this is candid, whether it would be fair to call us that or not.'

Elspeth spoke for the first time since she had come to the woman's bed. 'We're not on duty, Sally. If this were duty, I wouldn't be here. But duty isn't very far round the next corner. It seldom is. In this case, it happens to be imminent. But if we can anticipate misunderstandings before they arise ...'

'You're Mrs Kenworthy, aren't you? Edward said in his letter that he liked you very much.'

'In that case, tell him when you write back,' Kenworthy said, 'that I applaud his choice in females twice over.'

But at that point there was an interruption. A young house doctor, the plastic and chrome of a stethoscope prominent in the pocket of his white coat, came and opened the door of Sally's bed-side locker.

'No, don't go away, I shan't be two ticks.'

But they had to scrape their chairs away to make room for him.

'Dr Caley, meet the Murder Squad.'

She was not to know how near the Murder Squad was. The houseman grinned, not taking much in.

'Hullo to you. I'm the Heavy Duty Rummage Squad. Can't trust these people.'

He began to turn the contents of the locker out on to the bed: boxes of tissues, bottles of Slim-Line Cordial, toilet water, books, cards, magazines and soap.

'My locker was searched yesterday afternoon, Doctor.'

'Since when both canteen and trolley have been reporting extremely good business.'

He set aside a box of chocolate, a packet of biscuits and a bag of cheese-flavoured potato crisps.

'Hey! You can leave me the *Weeny-bicks*. They're low calorie.'

'Not *low* calorie, in your case, Mrs Hammond, *no* calorie, between dietitian's meals.'

'But Doctor, I wake hungry in the night.'

'In that case, I suggest you chew the tapes of your bed-cap. You're a naughty patient, Mrs Hammond.'

'And you have a cruel streak in you, Dr Caley.'

'I know, that's why I chose medicine.'

Elspeth bent forward.

'All right, Doctor, I'll put the things back.'

The houseman collected his contraband. 'I take it you're donating this to the Junior Medical Staff Common Room. Or it can go to the Welfare Pool, in which case you can be credited with it. Though, as you know, Dr Clements does occasionally cast an eye down the list.'

'Life in here,' Sally Hammond said, 'is a perpetual challenge.'

She laughed again: the dividing line between gaiety and bitterness was a very delicate one.

'How long have you actually known Edward Milner?'

She continued to smile. 'You know nothing, do you, Mr Kenworthy?'

'My mind is a virgin page.'

'And you want me to deflower it for you? All right. It will help to while away the morning. Give me a cigarette.'

'You are allowed those?'

'Now whose side are you on?'

And when she was settled ready to talk, she did talk, fluently and amiably.

'I've known him three years—*known* him, that is. After the war he came looking for me, round the villages, in the post offices and pubs. If I'd been free, and if I'd given him the slightest encouragement, he was clearly all set to sweep me off my feet. But even if I'd been unattached and studying the field, I think I'd have warned him off. It's only when you've reached my age and the state I'm in that you appreciate the likes of Edward Milner.

'However: when he found that I was married, and homebound, he didn't press himself. Edward Milner wouldn't. I don't know how disappointed he was, he must surely have more than half expected it. And perhaps you'll think I was rather a fast young lady when I say what I'm going to say, and perhaps you've already come across evidence enough to support that idea. Actually, I was rather a prim young matron, very proper indeed, with a highly romantic notion of my own faithfulness. But I would have liked Edward just a little bit more if he'd made some sort of pass at me; or, at least, if he'd shown that he'd have liked to. But, Edward, he's just too correct to live. I haven't ever seen that bachelor kitchen of his, but I can imagine what it's like.

'Funny, isn't it, talking like this about the man you're in love with? Oh, yes, I *am* in love with him. I'll sign that statement at the bottom of every page. How could I not be?

'But as soon as he saw that I was married, and had a growing son, Edward very properly withdrew—with dignity. He wrote at Christmas, sent little presents for Julian—that's my boy—sent me a card on my birthday, he knew the date, very often he's unexpectedly on the ball, is Edward. But he didn't actually ever come over to see me again, not for over twenty years, not till I wrote and told him I was in here, after the accident.'

She blew cigarette-ash off her sheet.

'I'm supposed to sit out in my chair to smoke. But they do their best in here not to notice an awful lot.

'Edward came to see me. Brought me a bunch of flowers so enormous it embarrassed everybody. And the best I could do in gratitude was burst out laughing. Luckily he saw the funny side of it, too. And it would be an exaggeration to say that he's been here ever since, but that's not far off the truth. You see, for the first few weeks, Brian, that's my husband, was over in Ward 9. They used to bring him over in a wheelchair, and pretty soon he was walking about the hospital under his own steam. Shaken up and scratched, that's all that happened to him. Whereas I, for the first month or two, well, I didn't want to know very much. When I was getting a little bit better, there was something I had to say to him. And if I had my time over, I'd say it again. Well, no; there are one or two things I wouldn't be quite so raw about. But I would say it.'

Cryptic; but now was not the time to stem the flow with questions.

'That was on Brian's first visit after he'd been home. He came the next week, too, I was almost surprised that he did. But then it went a fortnight, then a month. I heard on the vine that he's found somebody else. I hope he has, for his sake. He's a good man. He was a very...'

She searched for an adjective.

'He was a very understanding father to a boy he knew was not his. One way or another, we'd made a go of it. We weren't on fire, but now and then one or the other of us would try to strike a match. There were a lot of things we both missed, because the other wasn't interested. But for the accident, I don't think we'd ever have gone our separate ways: we'd ended up by standing still as of habit. We'd never really quarrelled even, because we were both too polite and too politic.

'Then Edward came along, and I let him know that the *Do not touch* notices were gone for good. I don't think he was much at ease, at first: a married woman. But he got used to the idea, before long. Perhaps he talked himself into it on some of the long drives back home. Since he saw the green light, he's been here every minute that he can. Of course, there can never *be* anything between us, but I think he almost prefers it that way. He doesn't take his annual leave, you know, he splits it up into little parcels of a few days each, especially in the cricket season.

'We go places together, you know. He pushes me in my chair round the rose-gardens, and we watch television in the day-room. This will be the third season that I shan't have missed a single over in a test-match. God, the game used to bore me to tears, but I think I'm keener on it now than he is. I look on it as a sort of ritual folk-dance. I know all the grounds: Trent Bridge, Old Trafford, Edgbaston. I even notice odd little differences in the individual score-boards, I try to kid myself I recognise the faces of the men behind the little peep-holes. It doesn't hurt me, you know, to see people prancing about in the pink of health. You'd think it would, wouldn't you? But we're nearly all the same, in this ward: show-jumping, athletics, swimming, the sight of other people using their bodies doesn't frustrate us. It liberates us.

'I can't explain to you what Edward has done for me. He's given me an identity, but it can't be for myself that he loves me, because he can't possibly know me, can he? I'm still to him something he thought he saw through a gap in the clouds and trees. And that's what I want to be. And, when I'm with him, that's what I am.'

'But he's getting to know you too, isn't he?' Elspeth said. 'And is still in love with what he has discovered.'

Kenworthy gently took the passion out of the dialogue.

'And you're with him, are you, in this obsession to get back among the stones of Yarrow Cross?'

'Not with him, no. I wish to God he'd leave it alone. But who am I to try to dictate to Edward Milner?'

'What's it all about? Do you know?'

'Something to do with the Prudhoes and those bloody Pascoes.'

'So Edward knows the Pascoes?'

'Of all the people from the village that he could come across, it had to be the Pascoes. But that's not surprising, really. Without doubt they're the noisiest.'

'When they're in circulation.'

'It's only Darkie who gets himself in gaol these days. Sammy and Tommy have been leading blameless lives for years.'

'So what is this tale that they've told Edward?'

'I don't know. It isn't even a tale. Edward says it's the key to something that would affect us all. I know this sounds unconvincing, Mr Kenworthy, but that's all I can get him to say. But whatever it is, he believes it. Which means that I have to treat it with respect, because Edward is a man who always minds what he is saying.'

'And he had this story from Darkie Pascoe?'

'Apparently.'

'And Edward isn't the sort of man whom Darkie would lightly take in.'

'That's what puzzles me. He's under no illusions about Darkie. Who could be?'

'So what's your theory? Hasn't Edward ever dropped the broadest hint? Theft? Blackmail? Someone else's crime? Someone else's family history—*your* family history?'

'Hardly. Edward knows my secret. If you can call a secret something that they knew in Yarrow Cross almost before I did—they did, you know. There were people there who knew I was pregnant before I did myself. Edward didn't have to go crawling under barbed wire to find out who was Julian's father.'

A tiny pause.

'Do you want to tell us?' Kenworthy asked.

'You mean you don't know?'

'Honest Injun.'

'Have people stopped talking, then?'

'No. We've barely started asking.'

'Mervyn Prudhoe. It never was a secret.'

'I see. So ...'

'So what Darkie Pascoe has told Edward can have nothing to do with that. In fact, I think it's just a load of nonsense. The Pascoes stole things. They always have stolen things. They're like magpies. They imagine tremendous fortunes in places where there's nothing.'

'You mean Edward's treasure-hunting? Surely he has more sense. Tell me, how come you were out of bed, the night Edward Milner flew over, Sally?'

'I'd been wondering when you'd get round to that.'

'Edward must have asked you.'

'He did. And only when he did, did I realise that it must have been the Pascoes. I didn't see them until later on, not when Edward did. They were at the side of my house—my parents' house. There used to be a little yard there, a paved space, where there was a well that served half a dozen cottages, including ours. The Pascoes were up to something there. Oh, I know you're bound to say that he could not possibly have known it was the Pascoes. Well, of course, he didn't. Edward didn't have time to recognise anyone, even if he'd known them in those days. He saw a pattern, with people in it: me at my window, men doing something over a well, with ropes, tools and tackle.

'And after his plane had bumbled away—I thought it was going to hit the church tower—I stayed at my window, daydreaming. Sad: thinking, believe it or not, that I'd never see again the figure that had waved. And he was a tragic figure, because only a few minutes later I heard the crash, ten, twelve, fifteen miles away.

'And I went rushing downstairs, shouting, trying to wake my parents, wanting the whole village to rush out to the rescue.

'I was mad. What could I hope they could have done? And that's when I saw the Pascoes scuttling home, with spades and ropes and rods. That's how I came to think it was they who woke me.'

'Sally-o! Physio!'

The physio-therapist, a grave girl trying to look casual, had come up with a vacant wheel-chair.

'There's no need to go away,' a nurse said. 'She'll be away about an hour. After that, we'll get her up and you can take her in the grounds, if you like.'

The physio-therapist lifted Sally from her bed with remarkable ease. Sally had learned how to relax when being carried, her face biddably at rest over the white-coated woman's shoulder while she was swung through an angle of ninety degrees. A nurse bent forward to pull Sally's nightdress down and lay a blanket over her knees. And in that instant, Kenworthy saw something that turned him physically sick. For Sally's torso was that of a robust, healthy woman, crowned by the smile and the open-air cheeks that could have been used as an advertisement for wholesome country foods. But from the waist downwards her limbs were wasted by the paralysis, the flesh fallen away from her thighs, the tibia tight as a steel rod under the bed-chafed skin, the kneecaps round and protruding, like those of some starving beggar-child in a charity poster.

Kenworthy looked away.

'You've promised us *three* steps today, Sally.'

And already someone was stripping Sally's bed. It would be waiting for her, smooth, cool and geometrically tidy, when she came back from the gymnasium.

'We shall want to spend much longer here, shan't we?' Elspeth said, a confirmation rather than a question.

'The Almoner, that's who I'll go and see, the Almoner. They get to know a lot, do Almoners. And I'd better start for Wiltshire directly after lunch.'

'I shan't come with you to the Prudhoes. I'll stay with Sally till you get back. Somebody had better be with her when she gets to know. I can't bear the thought of what it will do to her.'

'The evening papers will do it. Somebody might bring a midday edition into the ward. They're so keen on racing.'

Elspeth sighed. 'It's almost beyond contemplation. I shall tell her myself as soon as I can screw up the courage.'

'You'd better find us a hotel in town. I shan't want to drive back to Norfolk tonight. And ring up Diana. I'm sure she'll forgive us for going absent.'

'I'll do that now.'

So Kenworthy went alone to talk to the Almoner, a tall and elegant woman who had retained her youthfulness and remained abreast of the contemporary world, whilst at the same time preserving all the graces of a more formal provenance.

He made no progress with her at all. She knew where the line was drawn according to the book, and with all friendliness, she drew it there. For her, policemen were neither friend nor foe; within certain well defined sets of circumstances, she was their ally. But this did not include off-duty Chief Superintendents, even those whom fate had singled out for passing popularity with the public. Kenworthy had been hoping for some time-saving side-lights on Sally's background, her family arrangements, the stability of her resources. For a new, and probably finely balanced view on Milner and his visits. But the Almoner retreated impregnably behind professional confidences.

How right she was; and how utterly charming, how invitingly sweet-natured; how hard-boiled with experience in her refusal to play ball.

Kenworthy met Elspeth again in the corridor outside the ward. 'No dice.'

'Oh, shame! A stunted harridan?'

'On the contrary. I could have bullied a hag.'

'Well, I've done rather better than you: a room with a bath at the *White Hart*. And Di sounded as if she couldn't care less. Sally won't be back in the ward yet, and there are one or two things I want from the car.'

Kenworthy turned in the direction of the main entrance, but his wife put a restraining hand on his arm.

'Not that way.'

'This *is* the way.'

'I'd rather we went round through the gardens. I want to see their roses. They've a *Fantin Latour*: I caught sight of it through a window.'

So they found a side-door and came out from the shadow of the red brick walls into surprisingly warm sunshine, air free from the pervading hospital smells of iodoform and lysol, varied by the occasional whiff of floor polish, cabbage water and coffee.

'I'm beginning to get cold feet,' Kenworthy said.

'Cold feet, Simon? You?'

'I mean about Wiltshire, the Prudhoes ...'

'They're nobody. Minor land-owners. Probably second mortgaged to the limit.'

'I don't mean their social airs. What do you take me for?'

'Sorry, Simon.'

He could not honestly explain, even to himself, the sudden distaste for the case that had come over him. 'I mean this whole unofficial status angle. Last night, I was sure I could pull it off. This morning it doesn't seem so easy. I'm not usually chicken, but a complaint from the Prudhoes wouldn't be all that easy to side-step.'

He might have felt happier if Elspeth had argued with him; but she put no effort into it. 'You know best. And is this all because of that Almoner?'

'Because she was so right, so very right.'

Elspeth stopped walking. They had come across no rose beds yet worth speaking of, though there were a few specimens in view in a grassed bay between the wings of wards. Four young men in wheel-chairs, all wearing bath-robes of striped towelling, were gossiping at an intersection of concrete paths.

'If that's how you feel about it, Simon.'
She touched his elbow. 'About turn!'
'I don't get it!'
'I'm sorry, Simon. It was a monstrous thing I was trying to do to you. I shan't blame you if you never forgive me for it. All I can plead is that I've never tried to interfere before. And this *is* our holiday.'
'I still don't ...'
'You will, Simon.'

And they went back into the building through the door by which they had left it. The heavy antiseptic fumes settled round them again. The floor was so highly polished that it seemed unsafe to walk on it, except in mincing little steps.

And when they reached the entrance hall, Kenworthy saw his name written in chalk on a smearily dusted blackboard. He was to call in the General Office for a telephone message.

'Again, I'm sorry, Simon. I thought that another half day's freedom ...'

'Don't give it another thought. If this means what we both think it does. I'm not as big a man as I thought, you know. I need the system.'

'It's the sight of that poor woman that's upset you, Simon.'

'Anyway, it's probably not what we think. Derek probably wants to check his memory on some detail.'

He went to the enquiry desk, and was taken behind the flap with knowing respect.

It was the Yard he had to ring. The Commander actually asked him if he would *mind* interrupting his leave. The Chief Constable had called for assistance. The officer in charge of the case had particularly requested Kenworthy. The Commander understood that he already knew something of the case. He said that without suggestion of tongue in cheek. Oh, and would Kenworthy keep Special Branch minuted with all major developments?

So that was it: Derek couldn't possibly have unearthed anything yet to make him change his mind. MI5 must still be stolidly pressing.

Kenworthy rang Derek, had some difficulty in chasing him round the county switchboard.

'Ah, Simon. Listen, Simon.'

'Just tell me what's new.'

'The sheath, Simon.'

'Dabs on it?'

'No. It was out all night in the dews and damps. And mauled about by the army. It's *where* it was found that's new: not thrown away at or near the spot where it was used. Chummy got rid of it while he was in full flight. The lieutenant picked it up within a few feet of where you and I had been lying doggo—*behind* us. It couldn't have been Milner.'

'Well done, Derek.'

He said goodbye to Elspeth in the car park.

'End of the only case we've ever done together, Simon.'

'*End* of it? I'm tickled by your confidence.'

'End of our team-work, I mean. I know my place.'

'Your place is with Sally. Look after her, Elspeth. Get her delving deep. Milner's not off the hook till someone else is on it.'

CHAPTER TEN

It was almost a relief, Kenworthy would hardly have believed it possible, to be back on the rails again, to know that the rules, old friends to be wheedled sometimes into compliance, were there to be rested on; to know that the system was behind him; the specialists waiting to leap into service before he could lose his temper.

Was this, then, why he had never been promoted to be the lonely man at the top, the man who had to run the system without drawing any sustenance from it?

No matter; there was a certain satisfaction in him as he

drove over a spur of the Cotswolds, then down amongst the chalk-soil valleys. There was a kind of satisfaction, spiced with the threat of perhaps entire defeat, that he knew at the beginning of every big case. Except that he was no longer at the beginning of this one; he was well into it already. He knew the elements: that doomed woman with the blithe but precariously balanced spirit. He knew that Sally Hammond had upset him: she had rocked him more than he would ever have dared allow, if he had been in on the case within the meaning of the act. He knew that the Pascoes were nothing: filth, dregs, the rot in the bone that could work havoc on surrounding tissues. And Milner? An eccentric, a superior eccentric, situation prone; a giant manqué, but fated for ever to end up involuntarily creating mischief?

And he knew that he had to have authority behind him to approach the Prudhoes.

One of them was the father of Sally's son. So why hadn't she married him? Because he wasn't free, perhaps, or couldn't (or wouldn't) make himself free? Or perhaps she had turned him down. Perhaps her pride, or judgment, had been stronger than the threat of circumstances. Perhaps at one time she had passionately loved the man she called Brian; certainly he must have loved her, to the exclusion of considerations that would have outweighed most other things with many men.

Kenworthy approached the Prudhoes without anticipating that he might possibly like them. And here, too, at the cost of time he could ill afford, he abided meekly by the rules. It was as if he had suddenly become neurotic about the need for orthodoxy. He kicked his heels for a long time waiting for an interview with a local Chief Superintendent who was out showing his silver stars and crowns at an agricultural show.

'The Prudhoes? Father and son; bachelor establishment. They have a married couple, by no means youngsters, to cook and devil for them. Farmers: but not on a large scale. Two hundred acres or so: no cash crops, and very little run of the mill marketing. Prize herd of Herefords, and some pigs; pedigree stud. They brought someone over from Norfolk with them, who manages the place from a farm-house on their outer edges. Quiet chap, who doesn't show himself much, and does as he's told.

'They don't do much of the work themselves, but it has to be done their way. The old man's well into his eighties, still what you have to call active, but that doesn't extend to productive work. The son goes very lame: Commando major during the war—Dieppe, Anzio, Normandy—wounded somewhere in Europe. Walks very badly, with a heavy stick. Looks as if it gives him a lot more pain than he'd care to admit.

'They entertain very little: a neighbour or two, once or twice a year. Nothing like the scale on which they used to live in Norfolk, so I'm told. I gather that out there the old man was very much lord of the manor. Nothing like that here. He was a county justice from sometime in the 1940s until he reached retiring age, and the son has followed him on the Bench. But they take things very quietly. What's your interest? May I ask? I gather there's been a bit of a barney, out amongst the heather.'

'Information, that's all. Case with roots.'

'I should think they'll do you rather well in an old-fashioned way. Drop in here for a drink this evening, if you're coming back this way. I'd like to be kept posted.'

The house was Victorian Gothic, perhaps on an earlier foundation. There was a bay window along the western elevation that might have been Tudor; but it had been mucked about with: crenellations, gargoyles, devices in mock heraldry that didn't co-ordinate with anything. The ground-plan was curiously octagonal, top-heavy, like a biscuit tin from the Great Exhibition. Behind the house stretched steadings that could spell out to a trained eye the history of stock-breeding into the age of technology.

Mervyn Prudhoe was letting out his bailiff as Kenworthy rang: a short, middle-aged, spare man, with an expression that defied definition; or perhaps there were no feelings there, no opinions, no self-doubt; a dirty felt hat, jammed tight over his forehead, a trench-coat, tightly and untidily belted.

'You'll speak to Coveney in the morning, then? Come in, Chief Superintendent.'

The house was full of antique pieces arranged without much sense of display; newspapers of the day and letters for the post lying on a refectory table. The rooms were high; there had been no interior decoration done for a very long time. One had the impression of great, cold, cubical spaces. For some time afterwards, Kenworthy was puzzled to put his finger on the source of his feeling of aggressive discomfort until it occurred to him that there was a striking lack of cushions. The only ones they seemed to have were those, drab and compressed, on which they were actually sitting. The curtains were long, heavy and colourless.

The two men sat on either side of an open chimney piece, in the middle of which was set a small red glowing electric heater, from which Kenworthy felt no benefit. Both of them had been reading: the old man from a middle volume of Toynbee's *History*; his son from *Pendennis*.

Mervyn kept within hand's reach, as the local police chief had said, a heavy walking-stick. He walked with great unease, halting and resting perceptibly at every swing of his stiff leg.

The old man was fleshless, dry and deliberate in movement, likely it seemed to achieve his century by the stringent economy of his movements. It was not lost on Kenworthy that his son made no attempt to introduce their caller.

'In fact, you'll be concerned in this murder in the Breckland. I read it in this evening's *Standard*. There won't be many mourners behind a Pascoe cortege, I fear. Though in all fairness, it's a long time since I heard of Tom or Sammy in any trouble.'

The younger man's tone was matter of fact; no offer of humour; but no pomposity; no suggestion, either, that he was particularly interested.

'Though, if I may say so, it surprises me to see you so far afield as this.'

'For information at the fountain-head.'

Prudhoe looked across in some surprise. 'I don't see that we shall be able to help very much.'

'Who better to talk about Yarrow Cross in the years when most of the seeds seem to have been sown?'

'I'm afraid we're going to disappoint you, Chief Superintendent. We hear a little information, from time to time. But it's usually months old, rarely reliable, and even more rarely interesting.'

'You don't go back there?'

'Never. We own no more land in Norfolk. And the Broads and coast have been ruined.'

'Does the name Edward Milner mean anything to you?'

Mervyn Prudhoe made it clear that he was going to be slow to answer this. 'Drink, Kenworthy?'

It was a long process, his movement across the room and back. And yet Mervyn Prudhoe was neither old nor ill-preserved. The pattern of his war-time service would put him in his early fifties, and there was a strikingly boyish look about him. His hair was black, short, frequently cut and fastidiously styled.

He brought his father, without asking his taste, a small glass of white wine. And while he was bringing his own and Kenworthy's whisky across, the old man spoke. His voice was neither faint nor cracked, but slow and unemphatic, consistent with the impression of niggardly husbanding of effort.

'It says in the paper that you're holding a man for this unpleasant business on the Heath.'

'I was asking your son about him. Edward Milner.'

'You'll have to speak up. I can't hear people as well as I used to.'

Mervyn took up the conversation. 'You're actually holding Milner, are you? A psychopath?'

'No,' Kenworthy said firmly.

Prudhoe examined the rim of his glass. 'Perhaps I'm using

the term loosely. A pathological case, at any rate.'

'He has an obsession, certainly.'

'If Milner has been charged, it isn't obvious to me what an officer of your calibre ...'

'How much do you know of Milner?' Kenworthy interrupted authoritatively.

'Only what I've read, and happened to remember, of stories in the newspaper. He's the man, isn't he, who trespasses inanely?'

'And who has formed an attachment for Mrs Hammond.' And how was Prudhoe going to take that?

'I did know that,' he said, without emphasis.

'And that isn't something that you read in the papers.'

'No.' It seemed, for seconds, as if Prudhoe were going to be difficult. But after a short hesitation, he resumed. 'You haven't after all, Kenworthy, yet asked me all the questions that you have in mind. Nor have I volunteered all you might like to know. I am not, I confess, at the present stage convinced of the relevance ...'

Kenworthy leaped a gap. 'You've visited Mrs Hammond in hospital?'

'Once.'

'Recently?'

'Not recently.'

Was he unco-operative, embarrassed, or indifferent? As if to answer this very point, he held his glass obliquely away from him in a sort of rhetorical gesture and made a rather solemn statement.

'For the record, Chief Superintendent, I have acknowledged my obligations. There is a long-standing settlement, dating from before the lady's marriage to her present husband. I would be the last to claim it is ideal. It would be arrogant of me to call it generous. But by material standards you would have to agree that it is acceptable. I accept the *status quo*, I think we both do, with some regret, but nothing livelier.'

'It seems to me that Milner is giving her all the emotional support that her condition needs.'

'That is my impression, too. I'm glad of it. And quite why you should think that Milner murdered Darkie Pascoe ...'

'We don't.'

'Thank God for that.'

'That's why I'm here.'

'I wish I could help you, then. But I'm afraid I can't.'

Behind them, high on the wall, were two portraits in dark oils; not Rembrandtesque, the shadows were mere shadows. And they had the effect of a whole ancestral gallery. It was like talking in the presence of onlookers. Prudhoe had a self-sufficiency that it was going to be very difficult indeed to puncture.

'I visited Sally Hammond earlier today,' Kenworthy said.

'How was she?'

'I left her in the hands of a physio-therapist.'

'A placebo,' Prudhoe said.

'You think so?'

'I'm sure of it. There's nothing much they can do for her. But I'm glad the N.H.S. doesn't stint such gestures. Her spinal cord, you know, was irremediably damaged.'

'In the accident?'

'Accident!'

His tone was sourness rather than contempt.

'But of course, you won't have had time to dig out that file yet.'

'Perhaps you could fill me in.'

'A nut sheered off in the steering linkage. They hit a tree at forty miles an hour. She was in the passenger seat.'

'Nasty.'

'The day after an MoT test.' Prudhoe let it sink dramatically in.

'The insurance company must have had something to say about that.'

'They did. They had to agree that no MoT test is a guarantee of positive performance two minutes after the vehicle is back in circulation. It's a filter for keeping obvious unroadworthiness off the road, nothing more. The mechanic swore that there was no play in the steering-box when he tested the car. There may not have been.'

'But you're implying ...'

'A charge of dangerous driving was brought against Brian Hammond to establish a verdict. It was, of course, thrown out. And certain facts were not mentioned in evidence.'

'Which you knew about?'

'As it happens.'

'And suppressed? Or were a party to suppressing?'

'A sin of omission. Nobody asked. And if they had, we could only have made things worse for Sally, who was an innocent party, anyway.'

'Innocent of what?'

'Of damned negligence. At least, that's the lowest at which I would rate it with any certainty. You might be able to make more of it.'

'Do, please, be explicit.'

'No. It will come with greater force if you unravel it for yourself.'

'I haven't time for parlour games, Mr Prudhoe.'

'I'm an interested party. And what I tell you is only hearsay. You'll have to go from me to source, whatever I tell you.'

'What source?'

'Go to the Threeways Garage, Pitney St Mary: it's about eight miles north west of the training area. A small forecourt and service station. The one where Tom Pascoe works.'

'Does he, by Jove?'

'Oh, I can see your eyes lighting up. Believe me, that has no sinister significance. Tom Pascoe is a mechanical genius, in one direction only: the internal combustion engine. I'll tell you this: if my garage couldn't diagnose a fault first time over, I'd as soon Tom Pascoe looked at it as any man I know. Or not look, listen. He can hear a sickness in a car in ten seconds, whether it's a whine in a bearing or a stoppage in a compensating jet. He's worth his weight in radioactive isotopes to the man he's working for. Oh, and incidentally, they don't use him for MoT testing. On paper he couldn't pass an elementary fitter's entrance test.'

'But I suppose he did most of the work on Brian Hammond's car?'

'No. He didn't. I may as well tell you but you'll have to do it all again from scratch, obviously. Hammond's car had failed its test at Downtown Motors. Two days later, he put it in at Threeways and it passed. Nothing had been done to it in the meanwhile.'

'So he'd shopped around. It's not uncommon.'

'It may not be uncommon, but it's irresponsible. Either Hammond didn't believe the Downtown report, or he couldn't afford to have his car off the road, or he hadn't the ready cash for stripping the steering down. In my view, he simply lacked the imagination to see what might happen. He sheltered behind a garage that skimped its job.'

'And none of this came out?'

'Downtown didn't come forward. They were not obliged to. Other people who knew kept quiet. Hammond kept mum. Sally, of course, was *hors de combat.*'

Kenworthy thought it over. 'Negligence, you said and nothing more sinister?'

'No. But it hasn't been investigated. And there could be possibilities.'

'Well, thank you, Mr Prudhoe. It's a pity ...'

'That I didn't set in motion something that might have deprived the Hammonds of their compensation?'

'I doubt whether it would, in fact.'

'At the best it would have involved them in a long and harassing wait when they'd plenty of other things to be harassed about.'

The old man leaned forward. 'You're talking about this accident that involved the Carver girl?'

'We are,' Kenworthy said.

'I do wish you'd wear your aid, father.'

'You know it makes me even worse.'

'What is your main source of information about Yarrow Cross?' Kenworthy asked.

'A service rather less closely knit than the C.I.A.'

Perhaps Prudhoe was not entirely humourless. But his lighter remarks were either poker-faced or purely accidental.

'From Robert Whittle, mainly, one of our tenant farmers, and I don't hesitate to say, our right-hand man. Dispossessed of his living at the same time as I was of mine. And one of my platoon sergeants, over the operative years. So I brought him over here with us. He still goes back quite often. He has hundreds of relatives.'

'They were flint-knappers for generations,' the old man said. Intermittently, his hearing seemed to be faultless. But his son continued as if there had been no interruption.

'You are welcome to go and see him. You met him on the steps as you were coming in. I think you would find him a very open individual, an irrepressible talker, with a fund of anecdotes, many of them pointless, about what it amuses him to call the royal and ancient days. Perhaps I should warn you in advance that his loyalty is unimpeachable. What he will tell you will be no whit different from what you learn from me.'

Again, was this dubious facetiousness; or was it a warning? There was something twisted and brooding in this fellow. Kenworthy was doubly glad now that he had not come privateering to this hearth. The consequences could have been historic.

'One wonders,' the old man said, 'if the eminent policeman of today knows what a flint-knapper is.'

'Roughly, I think,' Kenworthy said. But the old man did not return his smile. No one had smiled since Kenworthy had come into the house.

'I was talking to a Norfolk colleague only the other day, and he wasn't sure whether there's a practitioner or two still left in Brandon.'

'Were there any other major questions, Chief Superintendent?' The younger Prudhoe was not interested in flint-knappers.

'I don't think so, at this stage, thank you.'

'And do you want to go over and see Whittle? I'll come over with you, if you like. It's not all that easy to find in the dark.'

'Thank you, but I hardly think ...'

Mervyn Prudhoe came to the steps with Kenworthy, stood leaning on his stick with its handle turned forwards from him, the opposite way from which most men would hold it. Only a little thing; was it part of an elitist pose?

An electric lamp over the porch was flooding the stuccoed front with pale light, accentuating black shadows. It was switched off before Kenworthy had pulled out of the drive. The home vanished into a bowl of darkness behind him.

CHAPTER ELEVEN

Kenworthy arrived back to Elspeth at the *White Hart* without having fitted in an evening meal. But the night porter, looking as if the feat was worth the tip of a life-time, managed to produce a bottle of light ale, well and truly *chambré*. And, miraculously, there was a small plate of flimsy ham sandwiches which another resident, now in bed, had ordered and forgotten.

The residents' lounge was now deserted: armchairs in turquoise brocade. A storage heater, behind the genuine andirons of the pseudo open hearth, was barely taking the chill off the room.

'Sally can talk, Simon.'

More than once, Elspeth had listened to a total stranger's life-story on a three-penny bus-ride—and that without asking questions. Kenworthy closed his eyes: he was not really tired; or, at least, if he was, it was in a pleasant fashion.

'It never was a show-piece village, Simon. Not a wall, not a cruck, not a gable-end worth bringing a tourist from the main road. Mostly red brick and clay lump. Even the church was hardly worth seeing: mostly nineteenth-century reconstruction. And as the building, so the population. Two flint-knappers ...'

'Ah!'

'But mostly agricultural labourers. Undemanding. Satisfied. A land-owner's dream. Not a union member among them. And if their wages were poor, they didn't seem to think they had the right to have it otherwise. Their cottages weren't bad. No sewers, of course. Electricity and piped water came very late in the thirties. But the Prudhoes kept the roofs in good repair. The gardens were spacious and the Carvers had a bigger patch than most: hardly enough to be labelled a small-holding, but enough for a hen-run, a pen of turkey poults, their own goat.

'And that's how almost everybody lived, with varying degrees of green-fingery. It was the rhythm of the land that shaped their lives. There was one seriously committed poacher: a man called Reynolds. Some said that he was the grandfather of the Pascoe boys, but Sally doesn't think so.

'There were two pubs: the *Angel* and the *Flintstone*, in traditional enmity, probably because neither landlord could make a living from his barrelage. Some men stuck to one tap-room all their drinking lives; others changed their allegiance from time to time. The Pascoe brothers were the only ones to get themselves barred from both houses simultaneously.'

'I suppose it could be considered idyllic—in retrospect.'

'Perhaps. Cottages smelling of the warmth of oven doors being opened. But they were certainly all the puppets of the Prudhoes. The place had a soul, that's how Sally put it, but it hadn't a will of its own. It didn't even seem to want one. They paid Prudhoe their rent and though they had to put it in his agent's hands, it was given back to them for two weeks every Christmas, providing that their book was clean.

'Prudhoe was Chairman of the Parish Council and its members were all his nominees. They never needed an election. Members were co-opted by a self-perpetuating nucleus.'

'An enlightened despot. That's what I've always wanted to be.'

'A despot, yes, Prudhoe I mean, not you. But enlightened? I'm not so sure. Neither is Sally. The old man had quirks and he could be immovable. He had a thing about telephone kiosks, for example, and he scotched any attempt to petition for one in the village. He didn't like buses, and had a devil of a fight with the Traffic Commissioners when they wanted to route a service through the village. He lost that battle and women wanting to shop in town no longer had to walk two miles each way to the Threeways in all weathers.'

Elspeth took a tiny sip of Simon's beer.

'They seem to have been contented, though. There were fun and games with Prudhoe invariably the master of ceremonies: a harvest supper that was an affair for the whole village, an annual concert, a children's sports, a summer fete for the Church of England Children's Homes, a ham, beer and cheese supper for the cricket team. Even the club ground was in a corner of the estate. He bought them their pavilion and kept it repaired and decorated.'

'He probably chose the first eleven, too.'

'I wouldn't be surprised. Everything he organised was very disciplined, very proper. Everything had its place. If some young blood fancied himself as a comic in the village hall, old Prudhoe auditioned him first, to make sure there was nothing to embarrass the Mothers' Union. A Cavalier at home and a Roundhead in the market-place, that's what Sally called him. There were high jinks, but they were high jinks to order. The Cricket Supper was the night for almost obligatory beer-swilling; and the women who had waited at table had to retire to the washing up before the first of the toasts.

'And that's the milieu that Sally grew up in in the thirties. I haven't got a very clear picture of her family life, she wasn't at her most informative when talking about her own father and mother. Involuntarily, I mean; she wasn't at all loath to talk about them, but they just didn't come over Either she was idealising them out of conventional loyalty, or she was too close to them to be objective.'

Kenworthy pushed away his empty sandwich plate. There were things he wanted to know quickly: what had happened when Sally found out about Milner? Had any significant news filtered through from Derek? He would have to get on the official net within the next half-hour. But he forced patience on himself; he hadn't seen Elspeth enjoying herself like this for years.

'Both dead?' he said, still referring to the Carver parents.

'Yes. Her father was an older man; as staid in his way as old Prudhoe, though on a different level, of course, and without pomposity. A quiet man, but capable of a kind of childish fun in his way. He died during the war: pneumonia, following his annual winter bronchitis. His wife lived until the mid-fifties, an unhappy widow. Sally was fond of her, is a bit mixed-up about her, perhaps because it wore a bit thin while she was living with her as an unmarried mother. More about that in a minute. She was not an easy woman, and after her husband's death, she couldn't settle to anything. But while he was still alive, and Sally was growing up, she was a woman of standards: she liked books, pictures, poems clipped out of weekly papers—trivial things, mostly—Beethoven waltzes on the cottage piano, things that did not find their way into other homes in Yarrow Cross. She had a flair for better things though, Sally says, she was never articulate *about* them.

'There was no outstanding reason why the Carvers should be considered better than anyone else in the community. Superiority was not a creed that young Sally was ever taught; indeed, *airs* were anathema in the household in the years when the child was feeling for her identity. But *airs* were not the same thing as grace and dignity. There was a discipline about the home that extended beyond the demands of routine, peace and quiet.

'The "superiority" of Mrs Carver was nothing that she sought or claimed. But it was something that the village accorded her, unspoken and unanalysed.'

'Like Sally in that ward,' Kenworthy suggested.

'I think that's just it. But there was one woman in the village who didn't subscribe to the popular trend.'

'Emma Pascoe.'

'It's easy for us, Simon, to have got a wrong picture of Mrs Pascoe, at least, one at variance with Sally's impressions. When Derek took us to talk to her, there was only one attitude that we could take. We saw an old woman to be respected because she's still self-contained beyond the age that most of us will reach, to be handled with care because she's physically fragile. To be agreed with partly out of sentiment, partly out of courtesy, partly out of fear of what an emotional hurt might do to her There are things about her that we found amusing and laudable: but will-power can be mere wilfulness, whimsicality may be sheer bloody-mindedness.'

'Sally has certainly talked you round.'

'Only because what she told me was credible and real. You must remember, Simon, that it's years since Sally saw Mrs Pascoe. She's ready to believe in the near-decrepitude, but she hasn't actually seen it. She only remembers a very different person: a loner who brought up three grandsons to be criminals.'

'Derek told us that she often co-operated with him.'

'Tactics that, Simon, not moral vision. What nearly drove her to the end of her tether was to see them grow up as stupid criminals. And she had a hatred of Sally's mother that went back deeper than any village history that Sally ever knew.'

'What form did this hostility take?'

'Malicious gossip. Making parties. There was a group of

crones who were very much under Emma's thumb, though they didn't always hold their ground when she wasn't actually there in the middle of them.'

'Speaking of the Pascoes I must get on to the Yard to send me a sergeant down from B Division, somebody who can read a poem in a nut and bolt.'

'You're on to something?'

'Something that has at least to be eliminated.'

Kenworthy got up and examined the thermostat controls of the heater, fiddled with a knob, but produced no noticeable difference.

'I'm taking too long,' Elspeth said.

'Not at all. Truth lurks behind details.'

'We come to summer 1940, then.'

'Ah!'

'Remember what it meant to us?'

Simon had been motor-cycle borne, a sergeant back from Dunkirk, troops thin on the ground along the south coast. Blue skies, hot sunshine. Battle of Britain dog-fights and vapour trails. Elspeth had come down sometimes at weekends. He had found her a bed in an erstwhile seaside boarding house. Against the backcloth of the unknown, invasion believed imminent, the threatened end of all known values, he had courted her. She was seventeen. Her parents thought she ought not to be travelling about Kent on her own. Sunday afternoons, corn ripening on the downs.

'It was an even more paradoxical summer in the Breckland,' Elspeth said. 'Even less immediately touched by the war—well, not untouched by it. There were men away, of course, an armoured division churning up forest tracks, but the rhythm of the heath still turned on rain and sunshine, harvests and drying winds. It was easy to feel the war was a long way away. For Sally Carver, Brian Hammond and Mervyn Prudhoe it was a very special kind of summer—restless, unfamiliar—full of all sorts of imagined symbolism, growing up, self-discovery.

'Sally had just won a place at Bedford College; she was

going to read English. Brian was going in the autumn—if there *was* an autumn, if the universities were going to open again—to Manchester to do chemistry. Mervyn had done a year at Cambridge, where he was taking the course in Estate Management. He was now daily awaiting his call-up papers.

'Sally and Brian knew each other well. They were of an age and had grown up together, though Brian lived in the outlying cluster of cottages known as Pegg's Corner. So they weren't exactly in each other's pockets every hour of the day.

'They had both won scholarships to the Grammar School some ten miles away. In that respect, they were quite exceptional amongst the village children. In those days you could count on the fingers of one hand the number of annual awards in that part of the county. There were fee-paying places, but these cost twelve or fifteen pounds a year, not gladly spent by Yarrow Cross, even by families who could have raised it, for the dangers of artificiality and disorientation.

'It was not an easy journey to the school. From the age of eleven onwards they had to cycle whatever the weather, eight miles to the Threeways Garage ...'

'Which keeps cropping up.'

'They parked their bicycles there, and caught a bus that deposited them in town half-an-hour before the school doors were unlocked. Sally remembers sheltering from the snow in a shed at the end of the playground, her fingers numb with cold.

'And the pair went through all the stages of adolescence. For the first couple of years, they hated their parents for insisting that they made the journey together both ways. In fact, they never sat together on the bus, and Brian would hang about looking unnecessarily in shop-windows, rather than be seen arriving through the gates with her. But they grew out of this in time. Sally remembers that it was in 1935 that they first became conscious of each other. It was the year of the Silver Jubilee, you remember, and there was a characteristic Prudhoe spectacular in one of his paddocks. Sally and Brian ran in the children's sports, but it was very clear to them how they had grown away from those who had stayed on at the village school. Many of those, in fact, with whom they had sat in the lower classes, had already left and were broadening their shoulders in the fields.

'Brian and Sally slipped away from the main celebrations and sat for an hour on a bank in a plantation of nursery pines, talking about their common world, with a new convergence of opinions and values. And after that they were simply accepted by the village as a pre-ordained and indissoluble pair. By the time they had been a year in the sixth form, they had branched out along very different tracks personally, but even these differences were a kind of agreement. They assumed that they complemented each other. During the holidays Sally loved to slip away amongst the scrublands with Lamartine or *Christabel*. Brian, as an embryonic scientist, developed a sort of mock-cynical materialism. They moved into a phase of almost perpetual dispute, but it was never a quarrel. I'm not wasting your time, Simon?'

'Far from it.'

'Could you hear that story and tell the couple that they never ought to have married?'

'I don't know. There are a lot of other things I'd want to consider too.'

'All right, then. Sally and Brian had a perfectly ordinary boy and girl friendship. They were fairly enlightened, by Yarrow Cross standards, but pretty orthodox, when you boil it down. They were mainstays of the Church Young People's Fellowship. They both taught at Sunday School. And their kissing and cuddling weren't far off puritanical: nothing that would have offended in the fade-out of a 1930s film.

'Then, in our Dunkirk summer, they got to know Mervyn Prudhoe. Mervyn had always been away at school, from the age of about nine. They had seen him from the village, but he had never mingled on the green, as it were. It was not, Sally insisted, through any natural snobbery on his part, it was the unquestioned order of life. His own pleasures, his absorbing occupations during school vacations, they took place naturally behind the fences of the estate not because he was imprisoned by them, but because within them he was fully occupied: with his tree-house in his younger days, his ponies, his twelve-bore and his breeding-pens, from which he was beginning to show beasts in his own name by the time he was sixteen.

'Once, when he was twelve or thirteen, he had fought and driven off a gang of village boys, the Pascoes among them, whom he had come across fishing in a stretch of brook that was formally, though not very effectively, private. The mêlée had its aftermath, because Emma Pascoe made all she could of it, and the agent made some discreet visits to pay for torn clothing. But what attitude Mervyn's father took in private about it, the village never heard.

'It was common talk that the father held the reins pretty tight. In his later years at school, when Mervyn started going in low in the batting order for the village eleven, he never stayed for as much as a half pint with the others after stumps were drawn.'

Sally's first meeting with him had come when she and Brian had wandered, one July afternoon, into one of the wilder corners of the park. Brian, in a passing enthusiasm for field biology had brought equipment to collect pond specimens. Sally was reading Jane Austen. Mervyn came up wearing cavalry twill breeches and slapping his boots with a steel-cored crop. They thought at first that they were in for remonstrations. Notionally they were trespassing, but did not really expect this to be taken seriously. However, one never knew. Mervyn Prudhoe had his reputation.

But he seemed to want to make friends with them. He questioned them about their school without much notion of what life in a country day-school was like. He showed a genuine and informed interest in Brian's specimens. He had read *Persuasion*.

The upshot was that he invited them to tennis. Brian did not want to go, and rationalised a hatred of all that Mervyn stood for. But Sally insisted, and they went. There were only the three of them, and the resulting mixed singles, ludicrously matched, petered out after a series of huge parabolic lobs into the hot, thick vegetation well outside the court. Mervyn could play a respectable game. Sally could not match him and Brian could not even begin to. Mervyn did not seem to mind. They sat in a summerhouse, sipped lemonade and talked.

Brian knew more about science than Mervyn did; but Mervyn could run rings round him when it came to agricultural applications. Sally had read more than Mervyn, but Mervyn's tastes were more confident. He knew more than she did about music and painting.

'As Sally put it, *he'd seen more originals*. And there's no doubt, Simon, he must have been a pretty shattering find for a girl. Well, even when she was telling me about it, sitting out in the rose-garden—I found *Fantin Latour*, by the way— she could half laugh at herself for her susceptibility. He was dark, athletic, classically handsome, witty, worldly, superbly poised and sure of himself.'

'And we've a pretty good idea what she must have looked like, too, half seen, for a split second, on a misty morning.'

'Sally didn't mention Mervyn's other attachments. There must surely have been some. God knows why he hasn't eventually married. Anyway, it was love at first sight and they both knew it. But for the rest of that year it was a very conventional relationship. Without being narrow-minded or priggish, they had a solid sense of propriety. Sally had had a straightish upbringing, and there's no doubt that Mervyn's code was pretty strict. They weren't ready to let themselves go—yet.

'It was all very sad, of course, about Brian, and rather untidy. At first he hung about, and could easily have become a laughing-stock. They made a deliberate decision to be kind to him, but of course it didn't work. It wasn't kindness Brian wanted. He stopped emerging from Pegg's Corner.'

But there was another source of hostility between the two

young men. Mervyn, with various O.T.C. certificates under his belt at school and university was a keen recruit to the Home Guard. Brian refused to join. He would do his military service in due course. At the moment his time was too valuable to him. He was going to be at a disadvantage in college, competing with people from bigger schools. There were gaps in his preparation, and he was sweating to get them filled.

Mervyn, on the other hand, was not entirely out of love with the war. He had some sense of his own destiny as a soldier, it was part of his own fulfilment. For him the war was not just a regrettable necessity. He believed in it, and Sally was drawn along to his point of view.

In the falling leaf of the Breckland autumn, the three of them parted. Brian went to Manchester, Mervyn to his regimental depot and very shortly after that to OCTU. Sally went to London where she had a few startling knocks in store for her. In intellect, in breadth of knowledge, in experience of people and the things that people do, she found herself a good deal less distinguished than she had assumed herself to be. It was one thing to have shone in a little school with only two hundred pupils. It was quite another to be amongst people to whom concerts and galleries were a commonplace; who did not think it curious that they had never visited Norwich or Bury St Edmund's.

Christmas 1940: home with a lot to talk about. And the men came back, too, Brian full of nothing but chemistry, and treating her with a somewhat puerile coldness; Mervyn with the white tapes of an officer cadet already on his epaulettes. She did not see nearly as much of Mervyn as she had hoped. For almost the whole duration of his leave there was a house-party at the Hall, strangers to her and, like Cinderella, she yearned for an invitation. But none arrived.

They met several times, however. One afternoon, characterised by damp, dead leaves and pale December sunshine, she was walking the lanes alone and he came round a corner on horseback. He dismounted at once, and led the animal by the bridle, and they wandered for a couple of hours, walking and talking. The next day they met without a horse, strolled round the unfrequented hedgerows of the Prudhoes' further fields, last spring's nests exposed in the black mesh of the blackthorn. They walked with their arms about each other's waists and kissed as they had last summer.

But now it was no imitation of the close-up of the film-set. Now they were aware of reality. She could feel the urgent privacy of his body; and he must have known she could feel it; and she stood and let him press himself against her. The blood swelled and tingled in her breasts. She felt the heaviness of her womb. And he started to kiss her as if he wanted to consume her. She clasped his mouth in hers, gave him knowledge of what she wanted.

But that was as far as they let it go—this time. She knew herself, and was honest about it. She knew they had reached a moment at which the only next thing was love-making unleashed and she wanted that. Oh God, how she wanted it. But there were other things one had to consider. There were things one could do: normal things, a spate of activity, at her dressing-table, at the sewing-machine, amongst her clothes and suit-cases, even about her mother's house-work, that could help to ease off the worst of it.

After that holiday, they corresponded, Sally more voluminously than Mervyn. In fact, in one given week, she was aghast to discover how much time she had given to writing letters as against essay-notes. Long letters, in which she spread herself at whimsy and at random: college gossip, college personalities, poetry, paragraphs quoted at length from books she was reading: Donne, Marvell and Patmore. She made Mervyn free of the sprawl and detail of her life; and his own letters, written on barrack tables and army bed-cots became longer and more personal. He began to look at daytime things through Sally's eyes, saving them to be reported on canteen notepaper in the leisure of the evening. She lay in bed alone at night and wanted him, tried to imagine the abandon and the ecstasy.

At Easter she came home again, but this time not the men. It was a terrible vacation, domestically a near-disaster. Her mother accused her of mooning, and asked her if there wasn't work she should be getting on with. For the first time, the women began to get on each other's nerves. For the first time, Sally realised that there was a gap between her and her mother that it was useless to try to cross.

'What is it you have on your mind? A man?'

'I'd be a strange creature if I didn't want, and have, men-friends.'

Her mother was working with her back to her, did not turn to face her. 'It isn't that young Prudhoe that you're eating your heart out for? You can forget *him*.'

Sally lost her temper. 'Mother—it isn't for you to tell me whom I should and whom I should not forget.'

'His father would never allow it.'

'Mother, what sort of world is it that you accept and admire? Do you think that Yarrow Cross's feudal class distinctions are going to survive this war? Do you think that Mervyn Prudhoe cares two hoots which side of the village green I was born?'

'I don't know what else there is for him to care for.'

'Mother, I don't know how you can talk like that. You don't know the man.'

Her mother turned round, then, and she was crying. But her tears did not soften Sally; they disgusted her, and she went off to do something in another room.

Another time it was, 'We've each got to know our place, Sally.'

'But Mother, the world is going to change. It *must* change.'

'There are things that you can't hope to change.'

'Especially if you don't even want to.'

'It isn't a question of what you want. Sally, I hate myself for saying this, but I must: Mervyn Prudhoe will leave you high and dry. He'll have to.'

Sally did not believe her. For days after that conversation she used one petty trick after another to prevent herself from being alone with her mother. She could not have tolerated a resumption of the topic.

Then a featureless airman waved from over the trees, and for a wild few seconds she tried to wake the village to run on foot to a disaster twenty miles away. There was no way she could think of of learning whether the rear-gunner had survived the crash or not. The holiday drew mercifully to its close.

One week in the following August the three central figures in the story were back in Yarrow Cross. Sally, to her dismay, had had a mediocre intermediate exam result: she had ploughed in the Chaucer paper. Brian had been called into the infantry within weeks of the end of his first college year. He positively hobbled in his army boots and his battle-dress sagged about his unmilitary shoulders. Mervyn had been gazetted, and was immaculate in the dark green beret of a fighting élite. Brian, alighting from the bus, and coming upon him unexpectedly outside the Post Office, had had to salute him.

The village was by now under its notice to quit. The population was being disseminated over villages and towns seven and eight miles from each other. It seemed equivalent to spreading them across the oceans. As so often in the face of intolerable catastrophe, it was the little things that loomed large: there were end-of-garden crops that the villagers were never going to harvest. The Prudhoes, who were reputed to have done very well out of the deal, were already deeply involved in their new home. Negotiations for it must have been going on for months before the rest of the village got wind of events.

Mervyn was going to spend half his leave in Wiltshire. His and Sally's opportunities were brief and overwhelmed by the fore-knowledge of parting.

They had one or two short and unsatisfactory meetings and then Mervyn took her not merely into the grounds, but in and about the Hall itself, where everything was in a state of chaos and movement: ancestral portraits being packed in crates, surplus furniture being marked for the salerooms. The house seemed to be milling with workmen, echoing with hammers, littered with packing straw and damaged plaster.

They came unexpectedly upon Mervyn's father, picking his way distraughtly along a corridor cluttered with tea-chests. And he knew Sally as he knew all the children in the village. He had always made a point of knowing each of them by name, only occasionally making a mistake. And he always tried to remember one salient fact about each child, so that he could put up an appearance of conversation: Robert Whittle, for example, had had croup when he was about six, so the old man always asked him about the state of his chest. With Sally it was slightly different; since she had won her university place, he had always talked to her about Meredith: a monologue that she was never able to turn into a dialogue, because she had read no more than a few anthology pages of *Richard Feverel*.

Now he did not appear to see her at all, walked past without looking into her face, but spoke to Mervyn.

'I want you to drive me over in the station-wagon to the Lowdens.'

Sally felt peremptorily dismissed. Mervyn leaped to do his father's bidding and made her no more than a sketchy apology. She went and wandered away into the fields, in the direction they had taken last December, wholly disconsolate, knowing there were only a couple of days left to them at the most.

It was a couple of hours before he came, startling her, vaulting over a gate with a boyish grin. 'The old man thinks we're seeing too much of each other.'

His tone showed a complete absence of any shadow of filial devotion. Again they faced up to each other; this time the signs were not to be withstood. He lowered her into the grass. It was a hot afternoon. 'We shouldn't ...' Mervyn said.

'Darling, I think we have to ...'

Elspeth took a deep breath.

'Sally said that she could feel the self-command ebbing

from her flesh as she said those words. Silly words; she knew that as she said them and yet she meant it.

'I'll say this for her, Simon: she makes no attempt to pretend that he seduced her. Nor would she have it that she seduced him. It was as it had to be.'

'And damn the consequences? Or hope against hope?'

'Simon, do you remember when you came back from the war, and we decided that it wasn't time yet to start a family? But it would be, very soon, when we'd got a few odd things behind us, like housing, and saving for furniture, and your examination for inspector? But after a few months had gone by we were more inclined, without coming to a positive decision, to let things take their course? Instead of taking measures, we were taking half-measures. Oh, Simon, you know we were. The night I conceived Peter, I *knew* we were doing it. I knew the tally—and I wanted it that way.'

'I don't think the two cases are at all comparable.'

'I do. Not in fine detail, but on a broad basis. It was the elemental versus the prudence of civilisation.'

'But we were married. We were so much more ...'

'I won't press the parallel. She wanted him. She wanted him to impregnate her.'

'To present him with a *fait accompli*?'

'Certainly not consciously. But it's deep in the elemental make-up of every woman. That's what biology is about.'

'It can never have occurred to her that he would renege.'

'Of course it didn't. But he treated her appallingly. In the event it worked out a good deal worse than even he had intended. He'd been posted to North Africa. I can't remember what battles there were that autumn, but she could hardly bear a newspaper or a news bulletin. And she knew it was likely to take weeks for her letter to reach him, telling him that she was pregnant and that she wanted to be. Then followed one of those terrible cruel strokes, one of those accidents that happen however well you've tried to plan things. This happened probably because old Prudhoe took the formalities into his own hands. She had a letter that she didn't even begin to understand for the first few readings: a fat wad of typescript that knocked her helpless when she grasped it. It was a draft settlement, for her comment and suggestion, from their solicitors. It arrived two postal deliveries before Mervyn's cavalier letter.'

'God! And he's been to see her in that hospital!'

'Once. I think Sally was still too sick to take it in properly. And I think she's got a reasonable perspective about it, now, in so far as you could expect any woman to. She's even sorry for him, because half his pelvis was shot away in one of the Rhine landings. You know how people gossip in hospital, and people who saw him have told Sally that there are things that surgical advances could still do for him. But he won't ...'

'You mean masochism? Conscience?'

'I don't know. You found him an odd man, didn't you?'

'A well-heeled oddity.'

'Yes. And the financial settlement was a handsome one, in so far as money and that kind of security are any substitute for what was Sally's real due. As she says, money did matter. In her initial rage she was tempted to turn the lot down. But that didn't last long. Commonsense soon got the better of hysterical pride. The son is doing well, by the way. He went into medicine, and when this happened to his mother, he switched to neurology. He's a registrar in a teaching hospital already.'

'And she married Hammond on the rebound?'

'It was not quite like that, in fact not like that at all. He wrote to her when he heard what had happened; he pressed her assiduously when he was demobilised. But she staved him off for a year or more. In the end, she said, she had to take him, because she knew she could trust him. And life with her mother *was* impossible.

'They've not been unhappy, not desperately so. Brian has always loved her, in his way, but he's an inhibited man. He's apt to dismiss what he doesn't understand. Aesthetically he has had nothing to give her. There are no flights of fancy about

Brian Hammond. On academic parchment he's a moderately qualified industrial chemist. But all he's ever done is routine analysis from stock production. He has no ambitions for anything more and he hasn't kept sufficiently abreast to make it if he wanted to. Sally's never let herself get into a state of abject misery about her lot. But she's always known herself as unfulfilled, not that that makes her an exception amongst twentieth-century women. The strange thing is, she feels she's been more contented since she's been bed-ridden.'

'That's an illusion.'

'And a merciful one with which Edward Milner has had a lot to do. But even there she finds herself in a dilemma. Characteristic Sally. She knows that it's finished between her and Brian. She thinks he's got another woman now and she doesn't blame him for it. She's glad for his sake. She says that there are things in Brian that could still be unlocked, but not by her. She'd like to give Brian his freedom. But if she does, Edward will press her to marry him. And for Edward's sake ...'

'She'll perhaps think her way out of that one, or be talked out of it.'

'I think so, too, Simon, but ...' She stopped. Kenworthy was aware of the silence and the brocaded lounge. 'I haven't finished. That poor woman ...'

Kenworthy could see that her eyes were not far from filling up. 'Darling!'

Elspeth composed herself. 'You've got things to do, Simon. It's terribly late. I haven't much more to tell you. Suppose we leave it till you come to bed. Go and do your necessary phoning.'

Kenworthy looked at his watch. He suddenly remembered with a terrible shock that this was his case now.

CHAPTER TWELVE

Late as his bedtime had been, and restless the night, Kenworthy was busy the next morning at an efficient man's hour in the headquarters office that Derek had provided for him.

Whilst shaving and breakfasting he had had an hour approaching panic. He had never let the strings of a case dangle so far. Damn it, he was in charge of nothing and nobody. There was nothing on paper; he had not even met the members of the hierarchy, above or below him.

But he felt a little better after he had met the sergeant whom the Yard had sent down for him: one of the new school of promoted young men, whom Kenworthy always found it difficult to get to know quickly: bespectacled, slightly intellectual, not given to a healthy ration of self-doubt, but quick, energetic and unambiguous: Duncan Tabrett. Kenworthy had never worked with him before, but had heard nothing to his disfavour in colleagues' gossip.

Tabrett had tabulated full-time and reserve resources. Manpower, transport, communications, specialist services: these had been listed and the necessary stand-by briefed. The woolly rolling ball of previous events had been reduced to the intelligible, if ruthlessly pruned, table of an official log. Derek, up to his ears in his daily round, was in and out all day, listening, suggesting, easing and lubricating. A technical bod was on his way this morning to try to make sense of a four-year-old fault in a steering-box.

Edward Milner was in the hospital wing of a remand prison; enough strings had been pulled for him still to be treated as Menschel's patient, and Menschel was dropping in to see him. Yesterday morning he had made one of those less-than-two-minutes appearances in the magistrates' court that people will block a shopping-street to watch. He had been formally charged on the stupid trespass issue, remanded for a week for further enquiries, medical attention stipulated.

But Kenworthy was determined that that week had to settle everything. There must be no more remands after that.

And first there was Kemp to be kept happy—the MI5 observer who had been waiting patiently since yesterday to interview him. He was too well fed and expense-accounted, too full of his own exotic (in his view) experience, almost too ready to express his readiness to co-operate. Kemp did not appeal to Kenworthy. But he did not look as if he was likely to be difficult.

'Well whose is he, Kenworthy? Yours, mine, or the trick-cyclist's?'

'I shall be surprised if he's yours.'

'So shall I. I've read all the back files. Milner's a nutter.'

'God! I hate that word.' And immediately Kenworthy cursed himself for betraying his feelings. He hadn't to have feelings.

'We don't like it, either. It makes it too easy to run for cover. Though with present day techniques ... I only hope that this man Menschel ...'

'Nothing for you to worry about there.'

'I'm taking a back seat, then.'

'Is that your brief?'

'My brief's open-ended. Keep me posted.'

'You can get what you want from Sergeant Tabrett, night or day. He doesn't leave that desk to eat or sleep.'

A dutiful thin smile from the sergeant: a superior bugger; Kenworthy would have to remember that his own sense of humour dated him.

A nutter. What would Elspeth have said about that?

Last night, before they switched out the bedside lights, she had told him how things had wound up with Sally. Distressing. But already Kenworthy was beginning to feel the impersonalising effects of distance.

Sally and Elspeth had been talking in the rose-garden. Suddenly the peace was shattered by a veritable tornado of wheel-chairs. A train of no less than five of them, furiously propelled, shot by them within inches. Some of the young men, immobilised in that hospital, many of them irremediably, had become adept at dicing with death down the long corridors and round the polished corners.

'Teatime!' Sally said. But she did not want to disturb their talk to go in out of the sunshine. Elspeth went back into the ward and borrowed a tray to take out tea, bread and butter, jam and cake. And while she was queueing at the trolley, she saw that someone had brought in the afternoon paper. There was a moment of semi-frustration, trying to read a headline that was being waved about in someone's hand. But there was no need for her to read every word of the two half-columns under the smudgy photograph of the Yarrow Cross barbed wire perimeter. Edward Milner's name was there. The item covered half the front page.

'Where were we?' Sally asked. They had been talking about Brian Hammond's disaffection.

'There's something serious that you need to know, Sally.'

Sally spread jam on her bread and butter, the plate balanced awkwardly on one knee. 'Greengage! One of our better days.'

'Sally, you were asking this morning why Edward was writing to you from a Mental Hospital.'

'I'll see his leg's pulled about that all the way down the ward when he comes on Saturday. He said he was using it as a hotel.'

'He isn't, Sally.'

A pause: Sally's knife in mid-movement; a toffee-paper blowing about the freshly hoed soil of a border.

'What do you mean, Mrs Kenworthy?'

'He isn't mad, Sally.'

'Of course he isn't. I know that.' Then the truth began to suggest itself. 'He's tried to go back *there*, hasn't he?'

'He's been back there, Sally, and somebody has murdered Darkie Pascoe.'

She did not have to say more. As Elspeth described it to her husband, it was like standing by to watch a woman die: not give up her last breath, but suddenly devolved from a fighting spirit to a diseased carcase.

'I saw the blood drain from her face, Simon, and it left her, not pale and harassed but blotched, stained and ugly. You wouldn't ever think of applying that adjective to Sally Hammond, would you? But that's what ugliness is: a complete absence of hopeful purpose. I could see how she's been fighting for months, cumulating into years, fighting against creeping collapse with a ferocious optimism and faith. *You promised us three steps today, Sally.*

'And she had only one thing to say to me, Simon. "You rotten bitch. Now I know why you've come."

'I started to say something else. But she just said, "Take me back to the ward." They put her back to bed. The weight of her head was too much for her neck to carry. The ward staff simply thought that I had over-tired her.'

Kenworthy picked up his watch from the bed-side table and remembered to wind it. 'Tomorrow when you go back there...'

'I can't possibly go back.'

'Well, who else do you think could hope to talk to her?'

'What on earth could I say?'

'That you and I and Derek are working flat out to get Milner off the hook. But that my guess is that only Sally can do it for us.'

Kenworthy watched Kemp leave the office. 'Co-operate with that man, Sergeant Tabrett. What I don't want him to know, I shan't tell you.'

'No, sir.'

He was still play-acting: he couldn't help it. Sour at himself, he reached for a sheet of paper, started to scribble notes of things he had to do, hoped to restrict them to a single side, Churchill-fashion. There was no order of priority yet. It was just as the ideas came.

Sally Hammond: Elspeth visiting.
                    Almoner?

Milner:	Charges and remand.
	Willing talk?
	Check precise movements since arrival Norfolk.
	How contacted D. Pascoe? Intermediary?
Menschel:	Check hospital staff: Milner's use of phone.
Threeways Garage:	MoT Test.
	Technical report; insurance co; police file on accident?
	Technical Sgt to see Downtown Motors.
	Tom Pascoe: relationship with Darkie?
Emma Pascoe:	Interview—aggressively?
	Village history.
Sammy Pascoe:	Present whereabouts. Worth interviewing?
	Relationships with Tom and Darkie?
	Village history.
Brian Hammond:	Assess.
	Worth seeing fancy woman?
	Village history. Cross-check on Prudhoes, Pascoes.
Establishment:	Vicar? Post-mistress? Policeman? Cross-check.
Prudhoes:	Interview when village history complete. Isolate old man.
	See R. Whittle, farm bailiff, preferably by surprise, without Prudhoes.
	Intelligence service—news from Norfolk?
Grenade:	Any references? Collections, military souvenirs?
Julian Hammond:	Views on mother's disability?
	Theories on car accident?
	Village history.

Kenworthy felt better when he had it down.

'Sergeant, have you gone into when we can get into the Battle Range?'

'They're willing to do all they can to help, sir, but they're hoping ...'

'They would be.'

'There's a NATO exercise, big stuff, with a skirmish at Yarrow Cross. Timing uncertain.'

'They're begging us not to mess up the march-table unless we have to?'

'That's the weight of it.'

'We have to, Sergeant.'

'The argument is that no one can possibly interfere with evidence while the place is under fire. They guarantee a cordon-guard while nothing is happening.'

'I want to get into that well today. Who's our contact?'

'Major-General, G.O.C. Blue Force, no less.'

'Get him on the phone for me. If necessary, I'll bring Kemp's masters down on our side.'

Derek came into the office, looked openly at Kenworthy's notes, put his finger separately against *Vicar, Post-mistress, Policeman.*

'Dead. Dead. Senile.' And he tapped the first entry. 'Don't worry on that score. Nobler heads than ours will fall, if any. Procedure agreed in a very high place. The press might possibly try to be clever, but they're pretty docile hereabouts. And Milner *is* under mental strain. I haven't heard yet whether he's feeling talkative this morning. So where would you like to start?'

Kenworthy looked at his list. 'Threeways Garage. Principally to see whether I can scare Tommy Pascoe. Can you drop a hint to them that I'm on my way?'

'I'll get a patrol to drop by and ask if you've been.'

'Your call to Command H.Q., sir.'

Kenworthy spoke to the General himself: hearty, business-like, obviously ready to stand up for reservations that he hadn't mentioned yet.

'We'll do what we can for you, of course. We're hoping ...'

'So am I.'

'How long are you going to need in there, Chief Superintendent?'

'Four hours,' Kenworthy said. 'From guard-room back to guard-room.'

It was a guess; it paid to sound precise. He hoped he was wildly over-estimating. There was a rustle whilst the General consulted papers; a whisper to some staff officer behind him.

'Midnight tonight till tomorrow first light. That do you?'

'Admirable.'

'Don't be late, Chief Superintendent. And make sure your watches are accurate. If they're not, a white flag won't be much use to you.'

'Mind if I don't come to the Garage?' Derek had the daily file of last night's break-ins in his hand.

And the sergeant asked a question with his eyes, his pencil still poised over his check-list.

'I'd rather not have a witness, this time.'

Kenworthy drove himself out there. The Threeways Garage was a single, low service work-shop, with shop-windows at the front: sweets and tobacco at one side, motorists' novelties and light accessories at the other. Kenworthy pulled up at the pumps on the central island. A bell had rung somewhere on the premises, but for a long time no one came, and the place seemed deserted. He got out and strolled about the forecourt: a breakdown crane with long grass growing about its hubs, a written-off mini, wheel-less, its bonnet in an incredible state. He went into the small parts shop: it was well laid out, not merely tidy, but clean. But no one in attendance. Crime Prevention needed a quiet word here. He could have filled his pockets.

He walked into the garage itself: tyre-pressure and lubrication charts, the console of an electronic tuning-tester—impressive, expensive. At the bottom end a mechanic had a utility van up on a hydraulic hoist, engrossed in the brake-drums.

Kenworthy approached unnoticed. He kicked an old brake-rod noisily along the oily concrete floor. A man came out of a lavatory, huge, barrel-chested, thick tangled hair and eyebrows that knitted down over the bridge of his nose in a permanent expression of menace, doubt and unintelligent apprehension. When Kenworthy had seen Darkie Pascoe, the features had not provided much of a model for comparison; but there was no doubting that this was Darkie's brother. Tommy was Darkie without the dead snarl, the bared teeth or the glazed eyes.

'Any hope of three gallons of four star?'

Tommy did not speak, but went straight to Kenworthy's filler-cap, inserted the nozzle and stood back, his eyes fixed firmly on the meter, as if expecting himself to be accused of giving short measure.

'That'll be two pounds twenty-five.'

'Have a look at my oil while you're about it.'

He did not need any; Tommy also unscrewed one of the battery plugs, stooped down for the bottle of distilled water.

'I'll bet that came straight from the mains,' Kenworthy said.

'We have our own deionizer.' Sulky; this man did not talk; he issued challenges from the corner of his mouth.

'Know who I am, do you?'

Tommy dropped the bonnet with a clatter that sounded symbolic. He straightened himself and looked Kenworthy in the eye. Kenworthy saw that his hands and fore-arms were trembling. Perhaps he was just one of those woolly-doll giants, an old English sheep-dog, a big, sprawling softie, like a Great Dane.

'Did you see much of Darkie in this last week or two?'

'None of us ever did see much of Darkie, did we?'

'Ever visit him when he was inside?'

'What, me?'

'I wasn't asking that row of bloody trees.'

Tommy sniffed, and scratched his chin with the back of his hand. 'What would I want to go visiting him for?'

'Buggered if I know. He's your brother, isn't he? Was, I mean.'

'Brother!' Tommy Pascoe said.

'Know where I can find Sammy, do you?'

'He lives in Thurrock, doesn't he?'

'All over Thurrock?' Trite, wasted on Tommy. 'I mean, can you give me his address?'

'Got it somewhere. At home.' Tommy thought it out. 'What do you want with Sammy? Sammy hasn't ...'

'Yes? What hasn't Sammy done?'

'Sammy's had nothing to do with us for years.'

'Must be a man of some taste, then. I notice you're not advertising yourself as a Vehicle Testing Station any more.' There was no blue sign with white triangles.

'That hasn't anything to do with me.'

'No? Had it anything to do with what happened to Brian Hammond's car?'

'Dunno what you mean.'

'No? Never heard of the case, haven't you? Don't know about a loose pin in the steering-train? Didn't see the wreckage, I suppose? Don't remember the to-do there was about it? They didn't come and ask you any questions?'

'I don't have anything to do with the MoT,' Tommy said. 'They don't let me.'

'There's still some hope for the poor bloody motorist, then.'

'Look, mister, I got work to do.'

'So have I. I'm in the middle of a patch of it this minute.'

'He doesn't know anything about it, officer.' A new voice; a short, underfed and worried little man who had come out of some office-cubicle; a threadbare blue chalk-line suit with a woollen cardigan.

'Perhaps you can help me, then.'

'Name's Hedges. This is my place. Get back to the Austin *Cambridge*, Tommy.'

Kenworthy watched Pascoe shamble away.

'Want to come inside? It's a bit parky out here.'

So they went into a dark office, dominated by naked women calendars, box-files of work-dockets and invoices.

'I've had about as much as my belly can stand of that business.'

'You'd better buy yourself some bismuth tablets. You're going to hear some more.'

'How long ago was it now?'

'Still within the Statute of Limitations,' Kenworthy said. 'I notice you're not on the testing market any more.'

'And it wasn't for that that they took it off me. Something quite unconnected. And unfair. That's the way they do things in this bloody country. Would you like me to tell you?'

'No.'

Hedges was the sort, Kenworthy thought, who would cultivate an aura of seediness and near-poverty, an endless complaint against the economics of supply and taxation, as a camouflage for his steady balance-sheet.

'But you can tell me about Brian Hammond.'

Hedges lit a cigarette, did not offer Kenworthy one. 'Brian Hammond came in here storming with a notice of refusal that he'd had from Downtown. Excessive play in the steering-box. He didn't believe it, and to tell you the truth, I had an open mind. Not that I went the whole hog with Hammond. He was convinced that they were all out to rook him, finding fault to keep their quota up and so that they could present him with a swingeing bill for putting things to rights. So would I have a go at it for him?

'There was no question, Mr Kenworthy, no suggestion whatsoever that he wanted a certificate round the back door. He knew me better than to suggest it. If the steering was dicey, then it had to be put right. So we gave it the works. Young Sid had a look, I had a look, Tommy had a look. Tommy!' Hedges opened the door and called across the work-shop.

'I thought Tommy was not an authorised tester?'

'That's not to stop us asking his opinion. Tommy, tell this gentleman about Brian Hammond's steering.'

'There was nothing wrong with it,' Tommy said. He was standing in the doorway, oil-grimed hands dangling in front of him. 'There was no free play at all.'

'Listen, Mr Kenworthy. Tommy has the strength of a

sodding gorilla. The way he shook those steering-rod ends, I thought he was going to dismount the whole bloody box. If there'd been a sheered-off nut in there, the whole bloody lot would have come away in his hand. I mean to say, *look* at his hand.'

Tommy looked down at it, too, as if he were surprised that it should be worthy of comment.

'All right, Tommy, back to work. Mr Kenworthy, if I could teach that bugger the difference between a decimal and a full stop, I could take on enough work to open a new wing.'

'Did you take the steering right down?'

'No need to. The Regulations state ...'

'Spare me.' Hedges wasn't the man to give away time and labour beyond the book.

'You don't think I wasn't upset by what happened, *bloody* upset. I was not working for strangers, you know.'

'I suppose not.'

'Those two used to park their bikes here when they were kids. I knew Sally's mother in the years when it wasn't coming all that easy. Her husband, you know, you could call him independent, but he wasn't bringing in much more than a labourer's wage. He had a rood or two more than most of his neighbours, but what did that mean, only more work? Two goats, milk to fatten his pigs. Have you ever been a slave to livestock, Mr Kenworthy? They're a bloody sight more demanding than petrol engines. And do you know how much of that work falls on the woman's plate?

'But she didn't relax her standards, didn't Emily Carver. She had a light in her eyes. She knew where she was never going to go herself, and that's what she had lined up for Sally. And who knows where Sally would have gone, if that young Prudhoe had kept his weapon to himself? Prudhoes! Don't give me Prudhoes! If that old bastard had negotiated a lease, instead of selling out in 1941 ...'

'What about the Pascoes, then? It seems to me you've been more than half the salvation of one of them.'

'Tommy? Tommy's all right. I mean, I wouldn't want to upset him. He might do all his thinking afterwards, if he bothered to do any at all. But we've managed to keep him happy many a year now.'

'And Sammy? Nobody seems to know a lot about Sammy.'

'Sammy opted out after one spell in jug. Sammy's got a woman behind him. Nasty, shrill little bitch. But that's what Sammy needed, just what he needed. And it wasn't exactly unfamiliar ground for a Pascoe to be toeing the line to a woman's voice.

'Everything that's happened to them has been the grandma's fault; but I suppose you have to make allowances, even there. She brought those three lads up single-handed after their father and mother died of the Spanish 'flu. Pity she didn't bring them up to something worth while. But she was too bitter, full of venom. When the word got round what sort of terms the Prudhoes had settled on young Sally, she nearly did her nut. She'd had it twice over, twice in a lifetime, that's what she kept saying, and nobody had ever paid her a penny. Those lads with no parents, and before that it had been their father, that she'd had by a Volunteer that she'd never been able to trace.'

'But by and large you'd say that Darkie was the only one who suffered lasting damage?'

Hedges closed his eyes in expressible disgust. 'Darkie? Darkie was the one with no bloody sense. He shouldn't have become a criminal, Mr Kenworthy. There ought to be a Careers Board advising such people against it. He hadn't the brains to pick a housewife's shopping basket. And yet the other two went with him, till I got hold of Tommy, and that thin-lipped, razor-nosed bitch from Dagenham got behind Sammy. And with Darkie away most of the time, enjoying the hospitality of the tax-payer, between us we've just about kept their chins above water. But when I realised that there were new shennanikins afoot ...'

'What shennanikins?' Kenworthy knew at once that he had been too sharp. Hedges stopped himself in mid-stream.

'What shennanikins, Mr Hedges?'

'All I mean is, when I heard that Darkie was out and about again.'

'Did you know that this man Milner had arranged to meet Darkie somewhere in the old village?'

'How was I to know a thing like that, Mr Kenworthy?'

'Had you ever met Milner?'

'Not unless he ever stopped here for petrol. And I don't ask them their names. As to that, I'd read in the paper of his nonsense, years ago. But I can't say I'd remembered his name. But when I filled Bob Whittle's tank, three or four days ago...'

'The Prudhoes' steward?'

'I thought to myself, that bugger hasn't come back just to see his cousins.'

'He was asking questions, was he?'

'He asked for petrol and I sold him some. He knows better than to ask me questions.'

'But you think that he was in the district to ask some?'

'What else?'

'Questions about what?'

'I don't know what goes on in people's minds, Mr Kenworthy. Least of all the Prudhoes.'

Kenworthy rounded things off quite suddenly. 'I've often found, Mr Hedges, that after a talk like we've had, a man sometimes remembers things that he thinks he ought to have mentioned. Here is my telephone number, personal and direct, if you have any after-thoughts.'

Hedges exchanged the compliment, a business card with the slogan *Service before Self*, from a small pack loose in a drawer.

Kenworthy went out to his car. Tommy was serving another customer, his eyes fixed firmly on the pump as if expecting himself to be accused of giving short measure.

CHAPTER THIRTEEN

'Not only is he not in a fit state to talk to you,' Menschel said. 'He's no longer even talking to me. I'll go so far as to say that when you were here before, he was pretty well in command of himself, except for the normal effects of shock. But in his present state of putting up a barrier against the world, he's beginning to stand in very real danger.'

'All the more reason why I want to be realistic about it. I promise you ...'

'Sorry, Chief Superintendent. He's too heavily sedated.'

'Yes. That's what you do to them. He was just about to spill the beans to us when we were here before. And you had to haul him off to take his barbiturates.'

'Largactil.'

'Let's not argue.'

'In any case, I doubt whether he had much more to tell you. It seems to me you'd pretty well got into his confidence. Or, rather, your wife had.'

'Touché.'

They were in Menschel's office again: the stethoscope on the desk, the photograph of his family, the window overlooking beech trees and squirrels.

'Mr Kenworthy I do want to help, both you and Edward Milner, but I think there's a total confluence of interests here.'

Confluence: not one of Kenworthy's own more usual words. Again, he was aware of the faint touch of accent in the psychiatrist's speech. It made their previous interview seem a long time ago.

'That's true. I'm convinced of it.'

'But it was bad enough for Milner to have witnessed that

murder—to have handled the corpse and the knife—without having to be accused of the act.'

'I'm sure you're right. But the only way to exonerate him is to find out who did do it.'

'Right and trite! How often have I found myself astride the law like this? And do you know, Chief Superintendent, I have in my time been known to serve both parties? Would you mind telling me, without bogging us down in too much detail, just how much he did tell you the other day?'

'Willingly.' Kenworthy turned back the pages of his notes. Menschel shifted his sparse and agile frame in his chair. Kenworthy dealt in staccato fashion with the main points.

'Precisely,' Menschel said. 'Not to put too fine a point on it, he seems to have told you, on balance, rather more than he told me. He seems to have been particularly expansive with you about what he saw from his turret.'

'Nympholepsis,' Kenworthy said.

'What the hell's that?'

'His orgasm in the clouds.'

'We have a different word for it.'

'You would.'

'It probably amounts to the same thing. But Mr Kenworthy I think I see the solution. I'll let you know the moment I think Edward Milner is ready for another consultation with your wife.'

Kenworthy was taken aback.

'Let him fancy that he is in love with her for a couple of hours,' Menschel said. 'I would think that your own position's fairly safe.'

'Dr Menschel, we shall have to play this very carefully.'

'We always do.'

Kenworthy was aware that there was something in the professional furnishing of the consultant's room that was very alien to his own walk of life.

'I don't mean professional prudence, Doctor, at least not yours. Mine. You do appreciate that we are talking confidences on the threshold of an open court?'

'I don't think that worries me much.'

'It does me. I can hardly have Mrs Kenworthy working for me at this stage.' He forebore to mention what he hoped she was achieving in the other hospital.

'Let her work for me, then.'

'God, Doctor, I thought I was bad enough.' But the ellipsis was too bold for Menschel.

'How, Chief Superintendent, *bad enough*?'

'I thought *I* knew how to bend the rules.'

'You bend them, Chief Superintendent, I make my own. Seriously: you do understand how little I can ever do for any of my patients? I can sometimes hope to put them in a position to help themselves. The first step is always to try to get them to tell us what is the matter with them. I think, now, that Mrs Kenworthy stands a better chance with Edward Milner than I do. He trusts her.'

'And she won't let him down. To a much more mundane matter, Dr Menschel. Milner made a phone call from here.'

'We have no hope of tracing that. I've tried. The Entrance Hall is always bristling with people. And it is true that the telephones are in arched alcoves that only give partial privacy. You can hear odd snatches, but only snatches. People have a habit of swinging about on their hips as they talk. And it is virtually impossible, unless it is so quiet that you can concentrate on counting the impulses, to tell what number a person is dialling.'

I'd like to have a look, nevertheless.'

'But certainly.'

Menschel escorted him down the broad staircase of what had once been a country residence, of which the Hospital Board had done their best to retain the elegant tranquillity: tall, leaded windows, with a family crest that could mean nothing to anyone any more, and a mid-Victorian newel post at the bottom of the banister. But the effect was partially spoiled by odd trifles of institutional necessity: the red-ringed press-buttons of the fire-alarm system, a hand printed notice begging for cigarette ends to be placed in the receptacles provided. And there was a busy traffic of faintly alarming individuals: a Lady Macbeth who assumed that her co-pensionnaires could see the same things in the middle distance as she could. They all knew Menschel; they were all pleased to see him; he had a way of cutting short their conversation without rebuffing them.

In the hall there were more of them: an old woman with her knees wide apart, knitting.

Someone was in long converse at one of the two telephones. Kenworthy had to content himself for a long time with examining the other booth. There were graffiti, some of them perhaps of considerable therapeutic significance: others less exotic: a bathing beauty with Cupid's bow lips. There were many notes of telephone numbers. There were heart-cries of love and hate, doodles of steam-rollers and windmills.

Kenworthy looked, and sighed, as so often in his life, for inanimate evidence to surrender its key information. In a certain type of detective story, some off-duty academic would find some way of doing it: analysing grease-spots, classifying material for a monograph on ballpoint spirit inks.

Kenworthy was looking for one particular number: but he would be the first to admit that he had no reason to be certain that Milner would have written anything down. He was conscious of Menschel, standing behind him, not crowding him, neither expectant nor unexpectant, ready to accept results without surprise or failure without contempt.

In the neighbouring booth, a girl in a red ribbed jumper turned with the receiver held partially away from her ear, looked at Kenworthy without really noticing him. She returned to her conversation.

'Well, no. Course not. Nobody ever tells you anything in here.' She put down the receiver; began to look up another number.

Menschel stepped towards her.

'Do you mind, Deirdre? Just two minutes.'

She pouted and moved aside, stretched out her arm for her bag after Kenworthy had moved into her place.

It was the same mixture: no bathing belle, but a highly imaginative sphinx; more steam-rollers and windmills. There still wasn't the number that Kenworthy was hoping for. Was it worth while isolating all the more recent jottings, assuming one could be sure of that, and looking them all up? There were cases in criminal history that had been cracked by application no less devoted. The front cover of the directory had been half torn away; someone had stood a hot mug of coffee on the exposed front page. Kenworthy picked up the book and fingered through its dog-eared pages.

Threeways Garage, Pitney St Mary.

The entry was in heavy type. Someone had made a little blue mark immediately to the left of it: a little blue mark made by a ballpoint pen, almost touching the letter T. It could conceivably be new. The back-room boys might have a way of finding out. But he wouldn't bother them. It didn't matter. It was inconclusive.

But it made up his mind for him. 'Thank you, Doctor, all yours. Deirdre.'

'You've found something, Chief Superintendent?'

'Enough to trigger off one of my more reckless assumptions.'

'I'll be in touch.'

'And I.'

Menschel saw him out into the grounds: gorse, broom, beech trees, rhododendrons, squirrels.

CHAPTER FOURTEEN

'Will you see Dr Julian Hammond, sir?'

'At once, Sergeant. Bring him in, and stay yourself.'

Sally's son had come without being called. Kenworthy studied him for some seconds without dissimulation. He would never have recognised him as his mother's boy:

resemblance to his father was arguable but not spontaneously apparent. He had dark hair, dark eyes, a rather sallow complexion. His manner was polite, almost suave, but carefully uncommitted.

'Have you heard how your mother is this morning?'

'I dropped in for a few minutes on my way over here.'

'How was she?'

'Low-spirited, with consequent clinical depression, but no immediate crisis. Your wife was with her and I wanted to ask you how official is that?'

'One word from you, or from her immediate medical adviser, or from the ward sister, or from my superiors, who don't yet know about it, incidentally, and she withdraws.'

'I can't see she's doing any harm. But I don't want my mother ...'

'There's only one person who has the final word for your mother, Dr Hammond.'

'And who's that?'

'Your mother.'

Young Hammond had a mannerism of holding his head back and thrusting his chin forward. 'That, Mr Kenworthy, is not wholly realistic. Fundamentally ill-informed. But it sounds good, and in spirit I find it admirable.'

'What I mean is that I'm desperately anxious to hold back from anything remotely undesirable.'

'Of course you are. But the point is, and the reason I have come to see you, is this man Milner.'

'You've met him?'

'Briefly. He has always been most pathetically anxious never to impinge on my share of visiting time. But that's not what I want to say. Your continued presence here, the fact that you're still treating this as an active case suggests that his guilt is not a foregone conclusion.'

'The only conclusion about guilt is announced by the foreman of the jury.'

'But you're hoping that it's someone else the jury will be considering?'

'That's roughly the state of affairs. Even as to the flavour of that word *hoping*.'

'I'm glad to hear it. That's what I wanted to know. He means a lot to my mother.'

They looked at each other.

'I know,' Kenworthy said.

'Oh, I know nothing about the man. Except that he flew over Yarrow Cross backwards whilst she was doing a balancing act on the window-sill.'

'Strange things used to happen in Yarrow Cross.'

Hammond smiled. 'Yarrow Cross, from the Anglo-Saxon *garw*, meaning noisy. Noisy Cross. Very apt. Particularly nowadays. Well, as I said, I know virtually nothing about Edward Milner. In a way, I don't even want to. The effect he has had on my mother suffices for me. After that accident, until Milner slowly asserted himself, she wasn't even trying.'

'You must have heard a lot about the old village as a boy.'

'Practically nothing. Of course, I never lived in the old village. By the time I was born, the inhabitants had dispersed. As a community, they never came together again. To tell you the truth, I'm not sure that they ever wanted to. There was some unrest, when the war was over, and the place was not returned to the people; but it nearly all came from outsiders: agitators, do-gooders, certainly not from those who would have had to up sticks again. They'd all settled to a new life, new homes, new jobs. They weren't begging for another upheaval.

'I heard stories: village catch-phrases, family jokes, but never a connected history.'

'And personalities? The Pascoes?'

'The only one I ever met was Tommy. He mended my bicycle punctures when I hadn't time or couldn't be bothered.'

The phone rang. Sergeant Tabrett looked over at Kenworthy. 'Sergeant Cottier.'

'I'll take it.'

Julian Hammond put his hands on the arms of his chair. 'I'll wait outside?'

'No. Stay. You might be able to tell me as much about this as Sergeant Cottier.

'Yes, Sergeant Cottier, Kenworthy here. Well, of course I don't know how you're going to tackle it. If I knew that, you wouldn't be here. Well, you've got the insurance assessor's report, and with a bit of grafting you might be able to go deeper into that than he did in the witness-box. And you've got the police reports. Oh, you have, have you? Well, that's something positive, isn't it? No, I know it's no substitute for handling the thing itself. No; I don't know any reason why they should. Must have gone to the scrap-heap years ago. No; I don't want you to go near there, not till I give you the clearance. That won't be till I've been there again myself. Yes, I do know what you're here for. You're here to do as you're bloody well told, lad.'

'You wanted me to hear that,' Hammond said. 'Mind if I tell you you're wasting your time?'

'Only too happy when someone's keeping a weather-eye on the clock for me.'

'Nothing to do with the car will advance your case for you. Just take the story you'll have heard at its face value. My father—Brian Hammond, I'm talking about—was furious when Downtown Motors refused him a certificate. He went to Threeways. They gave him one. I'm quite sure they shouldn't have done. Downtown were right. My mother thought so, too. She wanted to have the steerage overhauled. She offered the money, because he was always nearly broke: they used to housekeep and run their everyday lives on his income. It always peeved him to have to have recourse to her "special" income. She's lying where she is because of his false pride. She told him so, as soon as she was coherent after the accident. She's never forgiven him for it. That was what finally folded them up.

'So, Mr Kenworthy, save your own and your sergeant's time about that car. It won't help my mother. That's all that matters.'

'To you perhaps. I'm going to be pressed to answer additional questions. But let us have the expert view of your mother's prospects.'

'Expert? I'm a mere beginner. But since you ask: if a patient can move one digit a mere inch, apply pressure of half an ounce to the square centimetre, there are machines we can devise to make life bearable: if a patient has enough mobility to cast a shadow on a photo-electric cell, we can put her in some command of her environment. My mother has more mobility than that, much more. But the basic question is whether one is a vegetable, or a vegetable with a mind and soul. She lost her mind and soul when she saw what that accident had done to her. It was Milner who found them again for her. That's why I don't care who or what he is. She only means to herself what she means to Milner.'

'So what sort of a future do you see for them?'

'Milner wants her to free herself to marry him. He wants to set her up in a flat, after future hospital training and using every penny of the capital he can raise and every pound that Disabled Persons Acts empower the community to spend on its chronically immobile. They would have every contrivance that's technologically feasible, including a lot of experimental stuff.'

'And you think that that would work?'

'I don't know. I know that nothing else could.'

Kenworthy hesitated: then plunged. 'And your adoptive father? You're sure that's finished?'

'It's been creaking for a long time. In my boyhood they were companionable. I think that was its zenith.'

'Prudhoe?'

'He settled his contract. He preferred his father's philosophy. Serves him right if he's stuck with it.'

'So that if we don't exonerate Milner ...'

'My mother will undoubtedly degenerate, and die. You won't help her by solving a riddle about an MoT test.'

Kenworthy turned to Sergeant Tabrett. 'Contact that technical sergeant again. Tell him to concentrate on Downtown Motors.'

Julian Hammond looked at him in bewilderment. 'Well, it's your pigeon. I hope I haven't rubbed you up the wrong way?'

'Not at all. I think we need to know everything. I'm not simply concerned with what people did; I'm interested in what they intended. Now back to Yarrow Cross. Past history.'

'I've already pointed out, no narrative. A kaleidoscope of impressions, many of them undoubtedly misguided: what they used to sell in the village shop, what school life was like in those days, the village sports, the cricket supper.'

'And personalities?'

'Old Reynolds, the conventional comic poacher. The Pascoes ...'

'What of them?'

'They hated the Carvers.'

'Why?'

'I don't know. It was one of those quarrels that went back so far both sides have probably forgotten.'

'Your mother never said?'

'How much can a son know about his mother under the surface? She never attempted to explain it. She hated them. So did my grandmother. And I knew both women well enough to respect their views.'

'Tell me about your grandmother.'

'She was an exceptional woman. Oh, I know I talk, don't I, as if I'm convinced that we were an exceptional family. To tell you the simple truth, I think we were. Certainly not every small-holder's daughter, growing up in the 1930s found her way to a university. That was due to her mother's nurturing, as was the fact that she was able to hold her own when she got there. My grandmother had a certain silent confidence. I remember her, you know, I wasn't very old when she died, but she'd made an impression. She had *knowledge* and I don't mean book learning. You felt that there was a philosophy behind her, that she didn't have to expound.'

'You mean wisdom.'

'I think so. It's not a vogue word these days, is it?'

'Wisdom suggests serenity. There doesn't seem to have been much of that between them in the first year or two of your life.'

'Women sharing a cooker.'

'Is that all there was to it?'

'You could hardly trust my impressions of those years.'

'So. Mervyn Prudhoe. You've met him?'

'I happened to be there on the one occasion he visited my mother in the ward. I'd tried to get my mother to talk about him, as soon as I knew the truth about myself. She hated him, of course, for what he'd done to her. Behind that, I think, she harboured a corner of over-romanticised memory. In what she told me, she was trying desperately to be fair. And to do that, she had to avoid saying very much.'

'And your own judgment of him?'

'I was interested, fascinated. You can imagine. He was extremely courteous, scrupulously correct, a little embarrassed, nervously taut. I went out of my way to show him that I wasn't going to explode. I think he was genuinely interested in me, gave me a vague invitation to visit them in Wiltshire. Of course, I'll never go. I had the feeling ...'

And nothing attracted Kenworthy so much as reluctance in a witness. He waited.

'I had the feeling that he goes about permanently in a state of being ashamed of himself.'

'Maybe he has reason enough for that.'

'Maybe. For myself, I couldn't care less. I have my own career, my own life. I'm not bothered by the past. Only the future, including my mother's future. That's why I'm here and at your disposal for anything you need. Though I hardly picture that I can be of much practical use.'

Brisk, balanced, sure of himself. And how much uncertainty, self examination and torment did that mask?

Kenworthy would like to have known. But there were a lot of things like that that did not matter much. When Hammond had gone he reached for a sheet of blank paper and drew a rapid sketch, bold and recognisable rather than artistic: a country cottage, lattice windows, a girl with hair about her shoulders; at the side of the house three matchstick men with spades.

'That's what it's all about, Sergeant Tabrett. That's the picture that was etched in Edward Milner's brain, something he saw at a turning point in his life, something he couldn't get away from, in concussion, unconsciousness, delirium. Any guesses?'

Sergeant Tabrett was too careful to guess, far too careful.

CHAPTER FIFTEEN

Tabrett was careful at their canteen lunch, too, because it was the first physical confrontation between Kenworthy and Sergeant Cottier. The technical sergeant had obviously been extremely and unguardedly rude to Kenworthy on the phone; a man, presumably, wrapped up in his own expertise, with cynical notions about a vaunted figure whom he had never met personally. So now was a moment of some sort of truth, across the shepherd's pie and off-white boiled cabbage. Kenworthy was capable of anything, from pulling rank to his own particular searing brand of *Schadenfreude*.

The two men met over the table as if nothing had occurred.

'I've been to Downtown,' Cottier said. 'It didn't take long.'

'No?'

'The trouble is they've been talking about this for four years; and just started talking about it again, in a big way. It's impossible to tell whether they're remembering the original case-history, or some of the things they've said about it since.'

'As ever.'

'Apart from that, I can give you no evidence, but I'm certain in my own mind.'

'I'll settle for certainty.'

'When that car went to Threeways for its second test, the steering was competent but liable to early breakdown. And it didn't need any rustic thug to half pull the guts out of the thing to know that. There was play on a rocker-bar, and the mechanic I spoke to had been able to feel it with his spanner. So either Threeways knew they were putting a dangerous vehicle on the road or they just didn't bother.'

'Thank you,' Kenworthy said. 'Go and fetch us three puddings, will you? I'll have the rice.'

He went back that afternoon, alone, to the Threeways. Blew in like a North African sirocco and closeted himself with Hedges and Pascoe in the office cubicle. Tommy remained standing, there were only two chairs.

'All right, Hedges, you told me enough about yourself this morning for me to know what sort of businessman you are. Easy money wasn't it, the car Brian Hammond brought in? I've forgotten how many guineas you get for a statutory test; but you earned it for sweet sod-all, didn't you? Because if Downtown Motors were prepared to pass it on all counts bar one, you weren't going to blow labour-time doing it all again, were you? Brakes, lights, suspension had all been done for you, hadn't it? Just have a look at the steering, Tommy, let's know if you find anything amiss. And you didn't, did you, Tommy? Didn't go wasting your own or your boss's time? What did you do, Tommy, drive it once round the forecourt?'

Tommy, frightened, bovine, stood with his hands swinging idly in front of his thighs. 'I tested it properly, I had the covers off.'

'He did,' Hedges interrupted. 'I said he was to call one of us if he found anything that worried him.'

'So what sort of a mechanic are you, Tommy? I know you're not accredited; but there was nothing under that lid that was beyond you. So what, then? You knew; but it only belonged to the Hammonds, didn't it, bugger them? Let those buggers slew across a kerb and fetch up against a lamp-post.'

Hedges started to say something. Kenworthy silenced him with the sort of back-hand wave that forestalled argument.

'Serve the buggers right, eh, Tommy?'

Tommy stood silent, his eyes resenting the unaccountable intelligence of the world about him.

'Serve them right for what, though? That's what I want to know. What have you got against the Hammonds?'

Tommy made an animal noise. He didn't, of course, know what he had against them. They had always hated the Hammonds, he and his grandmother and his brothers. There were people you believed were against you, so you were against them. Things had never been different. It wasn't a thing you ever questioned; it was there. It always had been.

'The silly young bastard couldn't even mend a puncture on his bike,' he said.

'A very good reason for sending his mother and father crashing into a tree.'

'This is all supposition,' Hedges said.

'Not all, but if you're wondering whether I've got enough evidence to bring this back into court, the answer is no, thank God, I haven't. But if you open your bloody mouth again without an invitation, I might start trying. It's Tommy who interests me at the moment, not you.' He looked up and over at Tommy with exaggerated distaste. 'So it was you, Tommy, that Edward Milner rang from the Mental Hospital?'

'He didn't ring me. I didn't answer the phone. Sid did. He give me the message.'

'Which was?'

Tommy looked first at Hedges, then back at Kenworthy. 'That Darkie was to meet him, he knew where, that night at half-past-ten.'

'I see. And did you deliver this message?'

'There worn't no harm in it that I could see.'

'How did you deliver it?'

'I told him, didn't I?' Tommy was perplexed. If he failed to grasp his first interpretation of a question, it did not occur to him to look for an alternative.

'I mean how did you get hold of Darkie?'

'I biked home that way, didn't I, after Darkie got home from work.'

'At your grandmother's?'

'That's right.'

'And what did your grandmother have to say about it, when she heard the message?'

'I got wrong.'

A good old Norfolk idiom: succinct, unambiguous. Tommy, one gathered, was wearily resigned to getting wrong with people.

'Why did you get wrong?'

'She said Darkie hadn't to have anything to do with it. She said it would bounce back on him.'

'And did you get wrong with Darkie, too?'

''Cause I shouldn't have said about it in front of the old woman.'

'But Darkie didn't think it would bounce back?'

Tommy raised a hand rocky with knuckles and let it fall again. 'You know Darkie,' he said.

'I don't, fortunately, a chance missed for ever, I'm afraid. So why was it going to bounce back, Tommy?'

'Dunno.'

The eternal negative. It was always a hell of a job trying to break a man who had no intelligence at all. To trap a man, you had to mislead him. But Tommy seemed unable to follow anywhere.

'To do with something that had been buried, wasn't it?'

'Dunno,' Tommy said.

'You do: you know. You do know. Because you helped them bury it, Darkie and Sammy, the night the bomber nearly hit the Carvers' roof.'

'That bloody near hit the church clock,' Tommy said in a burst of sudden cheerfulness. Perhaps he was elated to be able to say something that was unlikely to be contradicted.

Kenworthy grinned at him, ready to play, if necessary, ready to laugh like an imbecile at the incident, if it would help. 'Did it now? Tell me about that. How near the church did it fly?'

'Bloody near hit it,' Tommy said.

'And what were you doing while the plane was flying over?'

'Well ...'

'Well, Tommy? You were digging, weren't you?'

'Not digging. We didn't have to dig, did we?'

'But burying something.'

'That was Darkie's idea.'

'And what was it you were burying?'

'He wouldn't tell us.'

'What sort of thing was it then? Gold bars? Jewels? Money?'

'Dunno. Papers, like.'

'What sort of papers? What were they in? A box? A suitcase?'

'A bag. They were in a bag.'

'What sort of a bag? A sack, you mean? A leather bag?'

'Waterproof. Like the soldiers had. Sort of wallet.'

'I see. And where did you bury this wallet? In the ground? Very deep?'

'In the well.'

'*In* the well? On a long cord, you mean? Or was the well dry?'

'No. That was three parts full. That always is, isn't it? They reckon there's a spring down there. We had to take some bricks out of the side, then put them back when we'd finished.'

Kenworthy took him over it all again, from several angles. How far down? Which side of the well, when you stood facing the cottage? Tommy was vague. If he did happen to know an answer, then he looked and behaved as if Kenworthy must be strangely lacking in reason not to know. If he didn't know, as was more often the case, he looked offended to have been asked.

'How often have you been to prison, Tommy?'

'That's a long time ago now, Mr Kenworthy.'

And the unfairness of the question was too much for Hedges' silence. 'Can't you leave that alone?'

'How long ago, Tommy?'

'Just after the war.'

'What was it for?'

Tommy blinked at him. It was even conceivable that he hardly knew. Certainly he wouldn't be able to recite the charge. Kenworthy had seen them: so obsessed by the irrelevancies in their defence that they never fully understood what they were trying to refute. Charged with X, Tommy would be busy parrying Y and Z, which hadn't been mentioned; pity the barrister who'd taken on a dock brief; only that poor sod had given up trying years ago. And some detective-constable or sergeant would have this chalked up as a success; it might even have been Derek.

'How long did they give you, Tommy?'

'Six months.'

'Did you like it in there?'

'That worn't too bad. That worn't as bad as I'd expected.' And then he added, gratuitously but bitter, 'That was all bloody Darkie's fault.'

'Oh, yes.'

But another image crossed Tommy's brain. 'I seen that on the bags in the yard outside the kitchen,' he said. '*Grade Three Pig Meal*. That was written on them. That was written on them bags. That's what they made the porridge with. That's why they call that doing porridge.'

'One other question, Tommy. How was Darkie going to make his way, that night, to Yarrow Cross?'

'I was going to have to take him, wasn't I?'

'I don't know. Were you? How were you going to take him, Tommy?'

'In the Austin *Cambridge*,' Tommy said.

'Bloody roll on!' Hedges muttered.

'I'll be seeing you, Tommy.' And Kenworthy took a last look at Hedges. 'You, too, I wouldn't be surprised.'

CHAPTER SIXTEEN

Emma Pascoe—interview aggressively?

Kenworthy's spirit failed him. He even doubted whether Elspeth had been right. It took a woman to know a woman. It also took a woman to go the whole hog the wrong way.

Was this the personification of evil, these rags draped on the spindly bones, those eyes lurking behind the mummy's skin? Or was she mad, unaccountable to reason, as Darkie knew no reason and Tommy knew very little?

'If she were my case,' Elspeth had said, 'I'd—what is the phrase you use?—I'd lean on her. She's sheltering behind her age, her decrepitude, but they're no credit to her. They could happen to anyone. You've got to respect them. But does that mean you've got to excuse them, too?

'I'd treat her rough. She won't die. She won't have a heart attack. Her body won't fail her because of an emotional onslaught. Her emotions don't work that way. She isn't normal, Simon. She doesn't move the way you and I do: from instinct to hope, from hope to motive, from motive to plan, and from plan to action.'

'How does she move, then?'

'From instinct to action.'

'You said she was intelligent.'

'She sometimes thinks up a clever plan. It's more likely to mess up the action than advance it.'

All very well. But there were disturbing elements of normality about Emma Pascoe that scuffed these theories at the edges. She had had an emotional shock; she had lost her cherished Darkie; and Kenworthy was reminded how far removed he was from his proper stance. He had no pity for the murdered man; only concern for the one who might be wrongly accused; and a stubborn temptation to be more interested in the motive than in the murder itself.

Emma Pascoe started crying the moment she opened the door and saw who it was: not tears of self-pity nor a histrionic screen behind which to shape the interview to suit herself. Those sunken eyes were smarting with rage; rage because if it had been anyone but Darkie, they'd have made a national cause of it.

Well, damn it, it was a national cause, wasn't it? The Yard was here.

But it was not possible to fool Emma Pascoe. She knew that they were thinking her instinct had taken her straight to an unalterable attitude. She looked at Derek with contempt; hardly looked at all at the W.P. sergeant, a blonde with film star cheeks and the inscrutability of routine duty. Emma Pascoe was prepared to deal only with Kenworthy.

'Where's the other lady?'

'She's on duty elsewhere today.'

Emma Pascoe looked for a moment as if she considered herself robbed. 'Well, have you got him yet?'

'A man is helping us with our enquiries.'

'Oh, aye? I've heard that before. You're not meaning the airman?'

It was as good a lead as any; Kenworthy let it develop.

'He's just a mug, Mr Londoner.'

'Kenworthy.'

'One who'd ought to have minded his own business. If he'd done that, none of this would have happened.'

'You think not?'

'Stands to sense, doesn't it?'

'Does it?'

Derek was sitting with his face slightly tilted, expressionless. The W.P.S. looked as if she had no feelings on any matter. Kenworthy reflected that he hadn't felt so affected by the possible reactions of his audience since he'd been an aide seconded from the beat.

'I don't know,' he said. 'I'm a stranger in these parts, still picking up the pieces.'

'A pity you don't go out to that other place. What is it they call it? Wiltshire?' She knew the word well enough, of course. It was beneath her dignity to show familiarity with it. 'Why don't you go there and pick up some of the pieces that are lying about there?'

'All in good time,' Kenworthy said affably.

'That's where the other lady is, I'll bet, in Wiltshire.'

'As a matter of fact, she isn't. She's sitting by a hospital bed, a rather nasty road accident.'

Emma Pascoe looked as if only a life-time of rubbing shoulders with the manners of the gentry saved her from spitting. 'A fat lot of good that will do her.'

'You are entitled to your opinion,' Kenworthy said. 'I happen to know the Prudhoes have been nowhere near Yarrow Cross for years.'

'And since when have the Prudhoes done their own dirty work?'

Ominously and irrationally, a spring clicked in the clock that had only an hour-hand. Emma Pascoe was wearing her dentures today. They were white, even; all the teeth looked the same size.

'Robert Whittle's been here,' she said.

'What, here to this house?'

And Emma Pascoe laughed, a dry rattle that was a stark reminder both of her age and of Elspeth's opinion of her. 'The day Robert Whittle sets his foot on my garden path, there'll likely be a murder that you won't have to go crawling about amongst the heather for.'

'Where and when, then?' Kenworthy asked.

'Two days ago. He stayed at the *Wheatsheaf* at Pitney All Saints, like he always does. Across the road from his own brother, his own family not being good enough for him. Yet all the same, they stick together, do the Whittles. You'll get nothing out of them.'

'Does Robert Whittle often come to Norfolk, then?'

'Now and then. He wouldn't be far out of sight if someone had told him that the airman was about.'

'No?'

'Well, what do *you* think?'

So it had to be amiable wheedling after all, the sort of soft soap that would have made Elspeth look slightly sick.

'I'm waiting for somebody to tell me.'

'What, me do your work for you?'

'It depends whether you want me to find out who killed Darkie.'

Her eyes clouded; if there was anything genuine about her, it had been her love for that man.

'So suppose,' Kenworthy thought he was introducing just the right shade of astringency. 'Suppose you save us an hour or two of work and start talking only about the things that matter.'

'Darkie thought he could handle it all himself.'

'Handle what himself?'

'Haven't you dug up that well yet?'

'That well?'

'Don't crack on to me, Mr Londoner, you don't know what I'm talking about. I lost my chance thirty years ago because Darkie thought he knew better than I did.'

'Something hidden in the well,' Kenworthy said, 'that Darkie was going to give the airman.'

'*Give* him?' Again the cackle, without a touch of mirth of any sort.

'Sell him, then.'

'For thirty pieces of silver? The Prudhoes would have given me four hundred, five hundred, a thousand times that much. But it's too late now. It was too late twenty years ago. I'll tell you what, I've lived half my life on the expectations of that piece of paper. But all along I've known, deep down in here, that I'd never touch it.'

Kenworthy began to see light. She was devious, she was dangerous, but she was vulnerable. She was a compulsive exhibitionist. It would be her undoing.

She fell silent, wanting him to question her.

'Blackmail,' he said eventually. 'That never came off.'

'When you see that piece of paper, you'll change your mind about a lot of things.'

'That's not how we handle blackmail. The one thing that we don't allow to influence us, is what's on the paper. We call the victim Mr X, and when it's over, it's forgotten.'

'This won't be.'

'A piece of paper? Let's think about that. Let's try to remember some of the relevant dates, shall we? A scrap of typescript, a letter, a copy of a legal document, a chit, an estate order from the Prudhoes to their steward. I suppose it wasn't Robert Whittle in those days? Showing the deal that old Prudhoe made with the War Office? Showing that he knew, back in 1941, that the villagers of Yarrow Cross would never come back to their native heath? Showing what *he* made on the deal?'

And Emma Pascoe laughed again, but now it was pure glee. He had played straight into her hands. He had given her best. He had shown her how utterly wrong and lost he was. Derek had raised his eyes a little, was looking at him keenly, but with neither expectancy nor disappointment. The sergeant with the blonde sheen and the Palmolive cheeks sat totally impassive.

What was it Derek had said, on the day of their very first drive through the forest? *A suspect's only got to keep his nerve, and he's got you beat*. Emma Pascoe wasn't going to lose hers. She wasn't normal. It was her nerve that set her apart. She was unbreakable. She was nourished by that piece of paper. For decades it had been the core of her being. Even now, until they dug it out and shook the loose earth from the folds of the wallet, it was hers. She would not be robbed in advance of that final moment.

'You evil old bitch,' Kenworthy said. He was towering over her. He knew that the rage was boiling out of his marrow. For a moment he felt dizzy with it, was sure that he was swaying on his feet, knew he had no hope of controlling himself. 'You foul old woman.'

Surely that woman sergeant must think he was going to

hit her? 'How much misery have you caused? And how much more of it do you think lies in your gift? What pride have you, except in your own power? And what power have you, except to ruin lives? What joy, except in seeing people suffer? What happiness have you left, except to wait for the next round of havoc?

'I don't know what this is about, Emma Pascoe, but I shall find out. You know I shall find out. You're waiting for me to. And it won't be anything I can put you in the dock for. You wouldn't mind ending your days in prison, would you, anyway, if you thought you'd delivered up your precious piece of paper? But I'll promise you this, Emma Pascoe: you'll not have your way, I'll see your rotten old bones out-live your chance to work evil.'

She had stopped laughing and was looking at him now: not apprehensively, not curiously, not enquiring. In her way, the black dots recessed in the folds of skin, she was staring him out.

And it was true as Elspeth had forecast: his furious verbal assault had not even quickened her heart-beat. She was proof against intimidation because she was afraid of nothing.

'Twice in a life-time,' she said at last.

'Yes: two chances. To do good or to do ill.'

'You don't know what you're talking about.' For seconds she continued to stare at him. Then Kenworthy took his eyes away from hers, not in defeat, not in scorn, but casually, relegating her to the limbo of those that did not matter.

'Come away,' he said to the others.

She started to laugh again then, a dry, spiritless rattle, a senile slow hand-clap of a laugh. She was still laughing when they closed the front door behind them.

For a long time in the car no one spoke. Derek concentrated on his driving and avoided looking at Kenworthy. The woman sergeant looked as if she could be trusted to remember nothing of what she had seen and heard. After a couple of miles Kenworthy leaned forward to the window.

'Over there, look! Isn't that a *muntjak* deer?'

CHAPTER SEVENTEEN

There had been magic of a sort on Yarrow Cross Heath on each of Kenworthy's previous visits; at least, a fallow mind could people the ruins with speculative figures. But tonight's moonlight was ineffective. It fell on crumbled walls like a memory of de la Mare; but no man in the party, least of all Kenworthy, was in the mood for phantom listeners.

For one thing, the party was too big. Kenworthy was determined that in the final revelation the group in the courtyard would be limited to the minimum of intimates: himself, Derek, Tabrett, perhaps the odd inspector from the Incident Force, if one was hovering. But in the initial stages it was a labour force that they wanted, and there had been no point in stinting it. Every able-bodied man who could be robbed of an off-duty shift had been mustered from local stations. Kenworthy had hurriedly drawn up the list of material equipment: spades, picks, flood-lights powered from Calor Gas cylinders. The cohort was noisy; he stamped irascibly on gossip and laughter; junior officers, anxious to impress him, were treating their men with unaccustomed curtness, exacerbated by the fact that men were working shoulder to shoulder who did not really know each other. Someone had suggested that there might be a contingency in which they would need a dog and one had been brought, no one now remembered why. It waited at its handler's heel, panting, disciplined, ready and happy to turn nasty to order.

And without being asked, the Camp Commandant of the training area had stood by a section of his normal maintenance squad, eager to co-operate. Kenworthy accepted them. They might be able to lay their hands on equipment that could save the day.

Kenworthy himself marked out the area of their immediate operation, extending a yard or two in all directions from the slab on which he and Derek had found the grenade. An owl flew off to find darkness and seclusion elsewhere, not a ghost with muffled wings, as one had been the other night; a mere owl, flying away from the unaccountable activities of men.

There was a moment of preparation, detailing the men, four of them, who were going to be the first to attack the soil. Greatcoats and tunics were folded over a wall and hung on the snag of a tree. The work was to be done within yards of the window in which Sally had sat. Even Kenworthy did not give it a second glance.

The first thump of a pick into soft earth: but within a minute their tools were ringing metallically. The area was, in fact, flagged all over: such soil as there was consisted only of weed-bound wind-sweepings, nowhere more than a foot deep.

'We ought to have brought a dowser,' someone said. But they hadn't; and no one was in a mood to be patient with otiose suggestions. They were going to have to lift the flags one by one. Kenworthy directed them to start with the one on which the grenade had been lying. There was no guarantee that whoever had put it there had known exactly which stone covered the well: it was extremely unlikely that he would have done. But a start had to be made somewhere, and once one flag was up, it would be easier to get at the edges of the others.

Kenworthy stood back to let the work go on. He was taking no part in the labour himself, tempting though that was, it would at least have helped him to be patient. He moved back under the shadow of the wall, began to fill his pipe.

Late this afternoon, he had called on Brian Hammond, successfully timing it to reach the house within minutes of his arriving home from work. Not unexpected, he had been treated with a respect in a house whose comfort and *mise en scène* were almost uniformly twenty-five years old.

Brian Hammond was a pale and embarrassed nonentity: embarrassed by the presence of his mistress, known to be such to an impersonally distinguished caller; embarrassed by what he had to admit about his collision with a tree.

'An appalling error of judgment on my part, the whole affair,' he said.

'Against which your wife had warned you.'

'I have chased that about my brain until it has become a fact of life.'

The woman who was living with him was ordinary enough: smart, but wearing nothing new, neither attractive nor unattractive. She seemed to have progressed from home-help to part-time housekeeper, thence to full-time and eventually to sitting tenant. It was difficult to know how much love she had for Hammond. They both behaved as if they expected Kenworthy to accept their situation with a carefully unspoken distaste for it: which was more or less the case.

Deadly dull, both of them: though hardly to be expected to scintillate in anticipation of some of the questions that he might have thrown at them. He let them off lightly, satisfied after a few minutes that they were roughly as honest as they were uninteresting. They told him nothing that advanced the case. They confirmed, unwittingly in many instances, a good deal of subsidiary detail; but much of which was irrelevant. Nothing they said contradicted, or even seriously qualified, the major impressions that Kenworthy had formed elsewhere. He felt some sense of relief as he drove away from their concrete drive: a little haven of suburbia, imported into the Norfolk rural scene. He did not know how Sally had managed to tolerate it as long as she had: how on earth she had drifted into moulding her entire life into this amorphous mediocrity.

Kenworthy put a match to his pipe. Smoking was strictly taboo to his lower echelons tonight, and he did not usually indulge in patrician dispensations. But he needed his pipe.

'Bit like a scene from *Hamlet*, Bert.'

'At least, they were supposed to be there for comic relief.'

Sorely tempted to tell them to cut the small talk, Kenworthy took a grip on himself. They weren't in any danger; they weren't in a tearing hurry; now that the job was under way, they weren't notably pushed for time.

He watched their silhouettes lever up the first stone, manoeuvre it to its edge, and after some fumbling and jocular cursing, carry it out of their way. One man, working alone, then applied himself to the patch of earth that had been uncovered. After a short while, Kenworthy emerged to stop them.

'We're looking for an old well, not digging a new one. There's nothing here. Move on to the next flag.'

The next one was easier to shift, but equally unrevealing. The third required a double attack, because it split into two from a stray blow with a pick. The man who was digging struck stubborn resistance.

'Another bloody flint.'

'Flint-knappers' benefit, tonight.'

'No, look, it's a brick.'

It was. In the further corner of this newest space lay brick and not simply loose brick. It was the outside edge of a circular coping.

'Sir!'

'Well, don't look so bloody surprised. We've never doubted that there is a well. It's just been a question of locating it. Now that you have, let's waste no time getting into it.'

It was relatively easy to uncover it.

'Mind you don't fall in, then.'

'Not likely to do that, sir, there's an iron grille across it.'

'So there is.' Kenworthy said it with forced angelic patience. The grille was less than a foot down from the top of the coping, well and truly embedded in concrete. It must have been put in as a precaution when the military first took over.

'Whoever did this,' Derek said, 'must have come across the cache or at least have disturbed it.'

'Not necessarily.' Kenworthy examined the mouth of the well. 'No, and this is not simply wishful thinking on my part. If they had had something valuable to put away, even the Pascoes wouldn't have hidden it as near to the surface as this. We've got to ask ourselves just how deep or shallow they would have worked, combining speed, comfort and reasonable safety. I'm afraid, however we look at it, the grille's got to come away.'

'Hacksaws.'

'That'll take a long time. There are twelve widths to get through.'

'We need an oxy-acetylene cutter.'

'Perhaps the R.E.s ...'

And here the army was able to help. They had the implement. They had the man who could operate it. Only he didn't happen to be amongst tonight's detail. He could be roused; and he was duly roused. The store-key could be located, signed for, and the equipment brought out to the scene. It all took time: foot-stamping, chest-belting, finger-blowing time. Kenworthy fell his policemen out for a smoke. He had the feeling that the steam had gone out of the operation. At last the cutter had his goggles on; the more recklessly inquisitive were ordered to stand back from the edge of the well. The next spell of the work began.

It was interrupted by a sudden hellish racket on the perimeter of the training area: small arms fire, explosions and yells of Red Indian high spirits. Something heavy thumped into the vestigial eaves of the Carvers' cottages. Bricks splintered. Something flew past Kenworthy's cheek.

'A dummy,' he said.

'Great relief!' Derek murmured.

The khaki members of the working party were the first to throw themselves flat to the ground. The rank and file of the police were quick in following their example.

'Something's gone wrong with the staff-work,' Derek said.

'You don't say!'

Another dummy shell. The man with the cutter abandoned his equipment unceremoniously, the jet of blue flame stabbing upwards into the night, and ran for cover.

There were the unmistakable signals of an infantry advance from a semi-circular line beyond the scrub-land behind them; light machine-guns, sub-machine-guns, and non-lethal but uncomforting thunder-flashes.

'There must be some way of telling them!'

'Surely the duty-officer in the camp knows what's going on.'

To have stood up and tried to signal would be to have courted several hundred times the odds that Lance-Corporal Davies had faced.

Then suddenly three balls of red fire shot up and floated gently down. The firing stopped almost simultaneously, except for a single belated rifle-shot. An armoured scout-car came tearing across the area that Kenworthy and Derek had called the prairies.

A young officer in a beret leaped out, a tough, squat man, webbing equipment over a ribbed sweater with leather padded shoulders. He was bursting with the energy of happiness and success, spoke in rapid, fluent, faultless English with continental vowels.

He pointed to one after another of the men who were raising themselves from the ground. 'You're dead! You're dead! You're dead! You're wounded in the chest! You've just lost your left leg! You will all please lie exactly where you are until the arrival of the stretcher-bearers, when you will be used to exercise the medical support services.'

One of the E.E.C. contingents taking part in the NATO exercise. For the moment, any interpretation of events was chaotic. The course of time revealed that the commander of this task force had been swanning across country all the previous evening, had broken through a cordon by a tactical trick, and had bashed through to storm his next objective without reference to the march-table.

Kenworthy walked up to him. 'Now look, sir.'

'You, my friend, are already dead. Please to lie down.'

'I am not dead. I'm buggered if I'm dead. I am a police officer.'

'What is this, police officer? This is Exercise *Resolution*, is it not?'

'Kindly take me to someone empowered to make a decision.'

'You are a spider, sir.'

There seemed to be infelicitous gaps in this man's knowledge of the language.

'I am not a bloody spider.'

'I make decisions. I make decision you are dead. You will please to lie down. I shall call umpire.'

A situation of prolonged and intolerable farce was saved by the simultaneous arrival of another scout-car and the duty-officer on a motor-cycle. A liaison officer with a white brassard eventually succeeded in drawing the Dutch officer from his world of professional fantasy.

There were salutes, hand-shakes, apologies and far too enthusiastic an interest on the part of all present to the job in hand.

The Dutch major seemed capable of putting his bounding energies into two worlds at once. 'First we consolidate. We prepare to meet counter-attack. Then we call for a tank to come and tear the grating from your well.'

'Counter-attack?' Kenworthy said. 'You don't mean to tell me ...'

The liaison officer had been appointed precisely for his ability to achieve compromise without deflating fictional enthusiasms. 'The counter-attacking force is still somewhere in Lincolnshire: it is unlikely to arrive on schedule, let alone get here early.'

A county inspector had a bright idea. 'Sir, instead of getting at the walls of the well from the inside, why don't we tackle it from outside the coping? It looks pretty solid, but I'm sure it's a botched job really. It shouldn't take long.'

'I'm sure you're right, Inspector, but we shan't improve our marksmanship by changing targets. That chap with the cutter was doing all right. All I want is the grating removed.'

'I call forward the tank now.'

'Tell him we don't want his bloody tank. Where's he

going to get it from, anyway? Salisbury Plain?'

Someone passed a hand microphone out of the scout-car. There was a spate of quick-fire Dutch. And already second waves of the assault force had begun to arrive and were casting off equipment to dig themselves in. More transport drove up. A motor-cyclist, standing on his foot-rests, bounced over the rough terrain. His engine sounded powerful enough to propel a battle-ship.

Chaos.

Kenworthy button-holed the liaison officer. 'Tell him he's free to do anything he likes. All I want is peace and quiet within a twenty-yard radius of this hole.'

The sapper signalled to those who were watching him that he was through another of the bars. The Dutchman came away from his scout-car, efficient, sweetly obliging. 'The tank will be here in five minutes.'

'We don't need a tank.'

But it came. It came thundering across the prairie and charged to a halt on the edge of the flagged yard, its engines idling with a roar that frustrated conversation and made the mere act of standing by a physical misery. The Dutch major waved to its driver to throttle down, but his signal bore no fruit.

The sapper, engrossed in his work as if he were aware of nothing happening around him, got up from his haunches to tackle the next part of the grating from a fresh angle.

'We need hooks and a tow-rope.'

'We need sod-all. We're doing very nicely as we are.'

'Here! Bloody hell! Look where you're going!' A constable leaped frantically for his life. The driver of the tank, pursuing some stratagem of his own, had decided to reverse and turn. With one track stationary, the other pulverised stone and rubble, crushed like a match-stick a spade that someone had left lying on the flags. The sapper leaped across the well, holding his roaring jet above his head.

And so the churning track thrust down over the brick coping of the well. The partially severed grating gave way under its weight. The nose of the tank pointed up to the stars as the rear sank deeper into the hole.

'We're going to need Heavy Recovery to get that out of here.'

But this was unduly pessimistic. The driver went into forward gear. His exhaust blasted out black, sickening fumes. His left-hand track was still on level ground, with perfect purchase. The right-hand track tore savagely at the coping, throwing fragments of brick in a shower across the yard. The tank pulled clear.

'Get it right out of here. Tell him to switch his engines off. Give him a cup of tea and a bloody medal and tell him to get out of my hair for just five minutes.' Kenworthy approached the damage. The whole orifice of the well was destroyed. The concrete that had held the tines of the grating had crumbled like dust. Whole chunks of it had pitched down into the bowels of the well, taking with it great wedges of the soil that had lain behind it. And even as he looked, a portion of the lower brick-work came away, depriving the upper layers of all support. Kenworthy jumped backwards. The whole mouth of the well caved in. There was an avalanche of soil and small solids, a splash of water, a stench of brackishness and corruption.

For one last moment of clinging optimism Kenworthy surveyed the remains of the night's work. It was all gone. Any cache made by the Pascoe boys had been disembowelled and its contents thrown down into the depths. Emma Pascoe's secret lay seventy feet down, under water, earth and rubbish, at the bottom of a shaft in which a man could not be asked to work until its walls had been thoroughly revetted. The task had moved now into the realms of mining engineering. At a rough estimate, it would take at least a week.

'Chief Inspector Stammers!'

'Sir!' The only formal moment in the whole of their collaboration.

'Form the men up and get them home.'

It was half past three when Kenworthy and Derek arrived home themselves. Diana was sitting up for them with hot cocoa and sandwiches which they were almost too tired to eat. She was wearing a long, heavy dressing-gown, severely tight at the neck. But she did not have much to say. She was in a mood quite different from usual: quietly sympathetic, asking no questions. It was almost as if she had had some sudden insight into the sort of thing that had been going on.

Elspeth was asleep, one out-stretched arm and a raised knee in his half of the bed. He did his best not to wake her.

But first he sat out on a chair to look through his notes. It was a habit of which he had never been able to cure himself, pushing himself on to more work, long after he was too tired to do any justice to it.

There were a lot of things that he could cross out now on his general check-list.

Threeways garage—Brian Hammond—Julian Hammond: There was no immediate need to have any more to do with them, unless something completely fresh blew up. He scribbled down a new agenda:

Sally Hammond:	Elspeth continues to visit.
Milner:	Elspeth to see.
Emma Pascoe:	Wait and see.
Tommy Pascoe:	Wait and see.
Sammy Pascoe:	See personally. Priority one.
Robert Whittle:	See personally, not in presence of Prudhoes. Priority two.
Prudhoes:	See personally. Isolate father. Priority three.
Grenade:	Keep looking.
Austin Cambridge:	Area to be searched for tracks when possible. Little hope.

He laid his notebook on the dressing-table, drew back the sheets. Elspeth stirred. Gently he lifted her arm. She woke, blinked once, and was wholly alert.

'Any luck?' she asked him.

'None whatever!' Then almost as an after-thought, 'You?'

'A lot of spade-work. We spent a useful day with Sally.'

'*We?*'

'Diana and I.'

'Diana? Good God!'

'Careful, Simon, she'll hear you through the wall. It's done her a lot of good, Simon, and she was very helpful to me. She's a lot less intense than I am. It made it easier to bridge the gap with Sally from yesterday's misfire. We were able to talk about trivialities at first. I managed to persuade Sally in the end that we're all on Edward's side.'

Elspeth twisted her body to re-arrange the pillows. 'And I've solved the main mystery for you, Simon, the blackmail papers. It's something that the Pascoe boys hid in the well, after they'd burgled the Prudhoes' Hall. It's a funny thing, that, because the Prudhoes were always very heavy-handed on the Pascoes: take them to court for a rabbit or a pheasant. But there was never a whisper of a prosecution over this.

'It's evidently a paper concerning the take-over by the War Office, something that would show Yarrow Cross just how they were sold up the river. Old Prudhoe could have negotiated a lease for the duration of the war. In fact that was the original intention of the powers that be. But Prudhoe, who was nearly everybody's landlord, preferred to sell out.'

'I'm sorry, Elspeth. It won't do.'

'Sally is convinced of it.'

'Emma Pascoe isn't. I tried it on her. She laughed herself silly.'

'But there's more to it than just that, Simon.'

'There'll have to be.'

'Sally's father was one of the very few who had a small free-holding. Not enough to negotiate in his own right, but situated awkwardly enough to throw a spanner in the works. And he was playing a double game, siding with those who were trying to get up a petition against the deal, but secretly signing deeds alongside Prudhoe. Obviously it was from

Prudhoe that the pressure was coming.'

Kenworthy considered it. 'If that's the case, I don't see why they had to bury the stuff. Why not just get on with the mischief-making?'

'Partly because the Pascoes never had much sense.'

'Always a rocky explanation. And senseless people are more apt to be impulsive.'

'Remember that Emma was behind it. And it was partly to wait until the men came back from the war.'

'It doesn't seem big enough, to me, Elspeth.'

'It could be big enough in the context of an insular community like Yarrow Cross, Simon.'

'And that's what Sally thinks?'

'She's sure of it.'

'I'm not,' Kenworthy said. 'Let's go to sleep.'

CHAPTER EIGHTEEN

There was no doubting that Sammy was a Pascoe: the same giant, hangdog frame; the same brow-knitting distrust of the world about him; the same facial suggestion that he would rather bandy thick ears than words. Only in his case there was a certain sandiness about his complexion. There was too much grey in his hair now for one to be certain how ginger he had been. He ran, however, to freckles, which formed great anaemic blobs on the backs of his huge, supine hands.

Kenworthy thought that it was probably a long time since Sammy had been in any kind of fight, or even looked for one. He had not exercised his strength for years. Civilisation had had its way with him in the shape of a car-body paint-shop in which he had worked for twenty years. The routines of shift-working, the statutory stoppages from his pay-packet, the world of shop stewards, strike pay and annual holidays on package night flights from Luton Airport had conditioned his being. His home, image of ten thousand others stretched between the factories and the Thames Estuary, bore witness to his pay-packet and the schooling of his tastes. He had a colour television set on hire, a mass-produced Belgian painting, with yellow willows that looked as if they had strayed from China. He had a shelf containing mostly paperbacks: detective stories of the tougher breed, also a Home Lawyer, a Home Doctor and a cookery book. There was a small garden, with a tiny square of lawn bleached and stained by incessant dog-droppings, a prefabricated wooden shed and a few rows of radishes, spring onions and lettuce in a keenly tended fine grey tilth. A heap of chimney-sweep's soot had been left out for weathering.

Sammy's inspiration to domesticity did not let him out of her sight while Kenworthy and Tabrett were on the premises. This did not worry Kenworthy. He thought, on the whole, that he was likely to learn more from her than from Sammy.

He would not have recognised her from the description by Hedges at the garage: it was some years since Hedges had seen her. But her nose was thin and pointed; her eyes, set abnormally close together, were of the sort that would give no quarter in any argument concerning ends and means. She would expect to have her will in major issues, never having given way on trivialities. Physically, she was one of those women who could not look well fed, however much they ate. And not having inherited a head-start in sexual attraction, she had not seen it necessary artificially to assume one. The Pascoe couple presumably enjoyed some things together, television soap-operas, and Saturday nights at the local. Doubtless they were capable of offering each other intimate titillation when they shared the mood.

Kenworthy came straight to a point. 'When were you last in Norfolk?'

'We never go to Norfolk.'

'Not even to look at childhood holiday haunts?'

'We didn't have holidays when we were kids.'

This was the tone of voice which Kenworthy had wanted to get Sammy using.

'But you have holidays these days, all right?'

There was a souvenir German beer mug on the mantelpiece, a costume-dressed Spanish doll, a Chianti bottle.

'Like I say, you can't take it with you.'

'Oh, don't think I'm blaming you,' Kenworthy said. 'I've got strong tastes for the homeland myself, but it's a matter of choice. What I'm thinking is you'd like to keep it that way.'

'I don't know what you mean.'

'I mean you've done well for yourself, Sammy.' Kenworthy nodded round the room as if he were jealous of it. 'You wouldn't want to lose all this.'

'And why should I lose it, Mr Kenworthy?'

'I'm quite sure, actually, you never would. I mean, after all this time, you wouldn't try running with the wrong lot again. When did you last do time, Sammy?'

Sammy's wife, her name was Grace, looked as if she were going to make the obvious interruption. Kenworthy wanted her to, but she held her tongue. He quickly discovered that she could influence Sammy without active participation. It was enough for her to be present.

'That's a long time ago, now,' Sammy said.

'And what was it for?'

The reply was not immediate. And it was softened by the inevitable floating question. 'We broke into a cinema, didn't we?'

'All three of you?'

Sammy did not deny it.

'Did you like it in the mush, Sammy?'

'That worn't too **bad**.' He had to show that they had not really got at him. His speech was still bucolic. Kenworthy wondered whether they ribbed him for it in the paint-shop.

'That wor better than the army. All you had to do was keep your cell clean.' Sammy suddenly broke into a broad smile; a new angle on a Pascoe. 'Didn't reckon the porridge though. Pig meal, that was. Grade three pig meal. That was on the sacks in the yard outside the kitchen.'

'Funny,' Kenworthy said.

'We didn't think it was funny.'

'No, I mean, I seem to have heard all this before. Tommy said he saw that on the sacks.'

'He *said* he did. He had it from another bloke in the same cell. It was a story that was going round.'

Five minutes more of this sort of talk, and they'd be good friends. Sammy had not slipped into confident fluency yet. His eyes were still restless, waiting for the trick that they were afraid they would not spot in time.

'Easy to get Tommy to believe anything, I suppose?'

'Well, let's be honest, Mr Kenworthy. I ain't got a great deal upstairs. None of us had. But I'd a sight more than Tommy. *Lard-head:* that was Darkie's name for him. That was the one thing Tommy wouldn't stand for. The times I've come between those two.'

'And Darkie? You let him do the thinking for all three of you, did you?'

This made Sammy ill at ease. He moistened his lips before he answered. ' 'Tain't right to be talking about Darkie. Somebody done Darkie in and *that* i'n't right.'

'I'm not trying to get you to say anything about Darkie that you shouldn't say, Sammy. But let's face facts. There's trouble you wouldn't have been in but for Darkie.'

'We didn't have to listen to him.'

'No. But you often did, didn't you? Like the night the three of you broke into the Prudhoes' place.'

Sammy was not ready for this. It knocked him off balance. He wasn't ready with any kind of answer. Kenworthy knew how his mind was working. Here was something that had never been officially found out; and here was a copper who knew all about it, after all this time. Sammy caught a distinct new whiff of pig-meal and he now said a silly thing: something he had read or heard somewhere, something that he had perhaps rehearsed in his mind, in some fantasy or other, something that he said with no tone of conviction whatsoever. 'I think I'd better have my solicitor here,' he said.

'All right, if you think you need him. I can't think why you should, though.'

A strained situation. Sammy was desperately afraid of ruining his chances by whatever he said next. He did not trust Kenworthy. Why the hell should he? Sammy did not really trust anyone, except Grace, he even thought he knew how to deceive her. At work, Sammy often did not speak from the beginning to the end of the week. He never had an opinion at a shop-floor meeting; there were men who took the mickey out of him, when he talked at tea-breaks. When they were on holiday, he did not trust his fellow passengers. People were quick to poke fun at Sammy.

It was better than the old days, anyway; he'd learned and remembered a lot of things from the old days.

And Kenworthy's presence here, sitting on the settee with his raincoat unbuttoned, was just too real a reminder of the old days, something that Sammy did think he could have forgotten by now.

All of which, approximately, occurred to Kenworthy too, as he sat looking at Sammy. He still waited for Sammy to speak. But Sammy could not overcome his diffidence.

'You don't think Prudhoe's going to lay a complaint after all these years, do you?' Kenworthy said at last.

Sammy still could not decide his next thing to say. Once, as a young man in amateur theatricals, Kenworthy had forgotten his part, had stood on the stage for an eternity, staring out into a dark bowl dotted with white shirts and pale faces, utterly incapable of finding a word to say. He knew how Sammy felt.

Grace came to the rescue. 'You've got to tell the man, Sammy. He knows.'

Illogical. It would have made sense if she'd said, 'He knows, no need to tell the man,' Kenworthy mused. This point had often occurred to him, because it was a point that interrogations often reached. How daft could people be, when you were getting the better of them with stupid questions?

Oh, come on, Kenworthy! Get on with it! Help the poor bugger. Ask him something he can answer. You can't expect the poor clot to tell the tale from scratch.

Grace was watching her husband expectantly; letting him know telepathically, perhaps, what he might expect from her afterwards if he were to muff it. Perhaps she was even trying to will a sign of tenderness across the room to him.

'Why did you break into the Hall, anyway, Sammy? What were you after?'

'Darkie had often talked about it. House full of gold, he said it was.'

'And was it?'

'Not that I saw. I mean, for anyone who knew anything about it, there was stuff worth taking—vases and things, paintings, silver. Well, anyone could tell which of the silver was worth having, and which bits would have got us found out. But stuff like that, you had to know how to get rid of it. I mean, Mr Kenworthy, in the Prudhoes' place we were out of our class.'

'So what did you take?'

And this stemmed Sammy's flow again. He could not see his way out of a damning admission.

'Honestly, Mr Kenworthy, we were there out of curiosity more than anything else. Tommy and I were, anyway. I can't speak for Darkie. Nobody ever knew what was going on in Darkie's head. We wanted to see if there really was gold all over the house.'

This rang true. It was the key to the Pascoes' mentality in their vintage years. It came from their basic relationship with authority. Through their glass darkly, it seemed to them that if a thing was illegal, or discouraged by society, then it must work to their advantage. That was why society was against it; because society wanted the pickings for itself.

'So what did you actually take, Sammy?' Pity to browbeat the poor sod like this. But this hurdle had to be crossed.

'Well ... money,' Sammy said at last. 'That's all we were after all the time, really.' He glanced furtively at Grace, needing her approval. Had he said too much already? Sammy was completely lost. He hated Kenworthy and the likes of Kenworthy. And yet there were things about Kenworthy that made him seem a decent chap, the sort of chap who might be good company in a boozer.

'Did you get any?' Kenworthy asked. 'Any money?'

'There worn't a great deal. Course, the Prudhoes were away, worn't they? Else we wouldn't have been in there, would we?'

'How much?' Kenworthy insisted.

This was how you'd know that Kenworthy was not just a chap in a boozer. He was a copper, wanting the naked facts, the ins and outs of a cat's arse-hole. You'd no sooner answered one question than he came up with another.

And it was naked facts that Sammy disliked talking about. He remembered how, after that cinema job, the detective in the witness-box had read from his notebook the exact amount, down to the last half-penny, that they'd found in the cash-box. These bastards always wanted it bang to rights.

'Fifteen bob,' he said. 'Well, fifteen and a tanner. That's all Tommy and I had. Darkie was supposed to have had the same.' He'd said it now. This must surely be the end of the paint-shop, the garden, the radishes and the garden shed. Sammy was certain now that he'd be going with Kenworthy and this other rozzer when they got up to go. And Grace was sitting there fuming, because he'd put his foot in it, because of something that he ought to have said differently.

'Did Darkie always do the sharing out?' Kenworthy asked.

'We wouldn't have been in half the things we were, if it hadn't been for Darkie.'

'Did he often swindle you, when it came to whacking out the takings?'

'We didn't know half the time what he was doing to us.'

'But you never thought of doing anything about it, you and Tommy?'

'Tommy and Darkie would have been at each other's

throats all the time, if I hadn't been there to come between them. Then we had to watch it, the old woman wouldn't hear a thing wrong about Darkie.'

'You found some papers in the Prudhoes' place, didn't you, Sammy? I want to hear about them.'

'Ain't nothing I can tell you, Mr Kenworthy. I never got to know about them papers. Nor did Tommy.'

'Just where did you find them?'

'They were in a desk, weren't they? An old desk. Well, I know now, you'd call it an antique. Like ... like, you might say, a kid's desk, in a school, with a sloping lid, that you could write on. Only it was nice, you know, not like a school desk, all nicely inlaid, with mother of pearl and that. Darkie had to smash it open to get in. I didn't have any hand in that, Mr Kenworthy. I didn't smash anything up. Darkie and Tommy, they were always for wrecking any place, before we left it. I remember the way Darkie prised open that lid. You could hear the hinges being torn out. In the end, the whole lid split right across. And then, when we got inside, there were lots of little drawers and things, all locked. That's where Darkie found the papers.'

A valuable piece. And Prudhoe, himself a member of the bench, hadn't even laid an information.

'What sort of papers?'

'I told you, I never knew anything about them.'

'What did they look like?'

'They were in a big envelope. With sealing wax on it.'

'And Darkie looked at them there and then?'

'He brought them home to show the old woman.'

'And what did she say about them?'

'She said there was a bloody fortune there for the lot of us. Only if we could wait a year or two, they'd go up no end in value. I've never seen her quite like it. I've never seen her so happy. She was bloody dancing for joy. Then she and Darkie had a lot of secrets about it. They often did, Darkie and the old girl. Tommy and I didn't get a look in. Then she and Darkie had a row. We didn't know the ins and outs of it, except that they had different ideas about how they were going to handle the stuff when the time came. Oh, Christ, it was bloody terrible. Tommy and I crept out of the bloody house, kept out of the bloody way. Then Darkie got hold of that envelope, and me and Tommy had to go with him, and we stowed it away, behind some bricks at the top of the well.'

'But you must have had some idea of what sort of papers they were. Darkie must have told you something about them, if only to keep you quiet.'

'There was something to do with land deeds. Something about selling the village.'

Square one.

'That's all he knows,' Grace Pascoe said. 'That's all even I've ever been able to get out of him. Give him a rest, Mr Kenworthy.'

Kenworthy turned and looked at her: the thin, fleshless nose that scarcely seemed to separate her eyes. 'There's one thing I don't understand, Mrs Pascoe. Whatever was in these documents, Darkie did the family out of it; and as things turned out, did them out of it for good. Only recently he's taken a chance to sell them off, no doubt at a knock-down price, to this airman. And yet Darkie was his grandma's favourite to the very end.'

'Birds of a feather,' she said. 'She admired Darkie, even when he was going against her. And who's to tell, with that woman? One minute she was egging them on, the next she was shopping them with you lot. All according to the way the wind blew. What's going to happen now? To Sammy, I mean?'

'Nothing, I hope.'

'You mean ...'

'I mean that all I'm interested in is who killed Darkie.'

'I wouldn't waste my time on it if I were you.'

'You wouldn't?'

'Bloody good riddance. I know that isn't the thing to say, but I don't care who hears me say it. Oh, I've heard tales.

171

I've heard enough to tell you what it was like, when they were kids. Darkie was just that little bit older than the other two, big enough to fetch them a four-penny one if they weren't going his way quick enough. *Lard-head*: who was Darkie to call his brother names? I wonder Tommy didn't have a go at him once or twice, from what I've heard. Perhaps he would have done if it hadn't been for Sam. He may not look like a peacemaker to you, but all that Sammy's ever wanted has been a quiet life.

'Talk about water under the bridge, Mr Kenworthy. Will this water never go under the bloody bridge?'

Kenworthy stood up, looked out of the window across the turd-spattered lawn, then beckoned to Tabrett who, he hoped, might possibly have learned something in the last hour.

Sammy still looked uncertain about his immediate future; or perhaps his was simply the look of a man who knows that he is about to be left alone with his wife.

Kenworthy and Tabrett left them to their quiet life.

CHAPTER NINETEEN

Kenworthy knew at once that Elspeth had been upset by her interview with Milner. No sooner was he home from his interview with Sammy than she showed by a meaningless answer to a question that she did not want to discuss it in front of Derek and Diana. Also at supper she was far from herself, a false and unsuccessful gaiety in conversation. And as can often happen when a husband and wife are on the verge of disagreement, it seemed unusually difficult for them to come alone together.

But at last Derek was called to the phone in the hall, and Diana went into the kitchen to put things away.

'Well, what happened?'

'We had a long personal talk, three or four hours of it. Nothing that will bring you any nearer to closing your case.'

'That's what you said for Derek's benefit. I can't think that he was impressed, either.'

'Simon it's intolerable. That man should never be being held in conditions such as he is.'

'A prison hospital isn't exactly like being a private paying-patient.'

'I'm not thinking of the actual medical conditions. I expect a patient in there gets all he needs, in course of time. It's just that he deserves something better than his present company.'

'Perhaps it will help him to have second thoughts.' It was not that Kenworthy was feeling uncharitable; he was impatient to get down to facts.

'It isn't that. He's in the next bed to a man who looks as if he's spent most of his life committing grievous bodily harm. And the two of them seem to be getting on perfectly, don't get me wrong, it's just that Edward Milner ought not to be locked away with criminals.'

'He's only got to undergo the tiniest change of heart.'

Elspeth was all nerves. She jumped when they heard Derek put the phone down, had one ear cocked for Diana's movements in the kitchen. 'And I couldn't stand the deceit of it, Simon. I mean, I didn't have to go in there in disguise, or anything like that. I didn't have to tell any lies. But Dr Menschel put a white coat on me, and stuck a clinical note-book in my hand. He said that that way I was less likely to arouse any unhealthy curiosity.'

'I don't think you'd ever really make a detective, Elspeth.'

'You don't think I have any ambitions in that direction, do you?' It was not so long since she had been insisting on comparable rank to his in the game that they were playing. He did not remind her.

'I hope, at any rate, you didn't have to talk to him in the open ward?'

'Oh, no. They put a little consulting room at our disposal. But people were coming and going all day. There'd been an accident in one of the work-shops. A man had driven a bolt through his finger and thumb.'

Derek came through to say that he was going back to the station for half an hour. Diana finished putting crockery away, came back into the lounge, spotted that there was some kind of unease between the Kenworthys, picked up a knitting pattern and went out again.

'Elspeth, what's the matter?'

'I know now what it's all about. Edward told me.'

'Well?'

'It isn't as easy as all that, Simon.'

'I hope you're not going to say you struck some sort of silly bargain with him.'

'Not a *silly* bargain, Simon.'

'Please don't misunderstand me. Any kind of bargain with a man in Milner's position would be injudicious.'

'Professionally, for you. My circumstances were quite different.'

'I see. We're not in partnership any longer?' Kenworthy felt himself becoming dangerously angry.

'My position is that I went there at Dr Menschel's request because, as he put it, he thought that I could get the floodgates open.'

'Which you did?'

Evidently Elspeth did not much like the metaphor as applied to something that she had actually experienced.

'You've told Menschel the outcome of all this?'

'In substance.'

'But you're not going to tell me?'

'Let me explain, Simon.'

'Before you go into all the complexities, just answer me one question. Do you now know who killed Darkie Pascoe?'

'No.'

Kenworthy felt some sense of relaxation. He didn't mind Elspeth playing out her psychological games, as long as there was nothing concrete behind them.

'Well, then.'

'But I do know who might have a motive.'

'And you're not going to tell me?'

'Do, please, stop trying to jump into the middle of the story, Simon. Let me begin at the beginning.'

He became stiffly silent. She could have the telling of it her own way.

'Edward made me make a promise. He didn't try to make me say I wouldn't tell you. He *wants* me to tell you. But in some way, he wants me to choose the moment, he doesn't want me to tell you until I can be certain that the information concerned will never come to the knowledge of Sally Hammond.'

'And don't you trust me?'

'Simon, I know you'd do a lot of heart-searching...'

'And not find one, you suppose?'

'Simon, as things stand at the moment she would have to know. Edward is sure that it would kill her. I don't go all the way with that—but I think it could do her inestimable harm.'

'So, I suppose, I would simply ring for transport and hare off to tell her?'

It was Elspeth who succeeded in entrenching herself behind a rampart of patience. 'No, you wouldn't. You most certainly wouldn't. But you wouldn't be able to offer any guarantees.'

'Because I'd have to chase up this motive?'

'Don't try to pump me, Simon. Otherwise I shall simply have to refuse to discuss it.'

Kenworthy got up and went and looked out of the window: a neighbour was spraying a rose that had not been planted more than a few weeks; another was upbraiding a salesman about a scratch in the door-panel of a mustard yellow brand new *Viva* that had just been delivered to his drive. From one of the houses a decent looking adolescent couple were setting out from the girl's home. A May evening; open-forecourt planning; green lawns, botanical tulips, fussy, and looking a little windswept.

Bloody women. Kenworthy felt a sudden surge of rage. Only three or four times in his life had he really lost his temper. He knew what it was like; he frightened even himself. It was a pattern he had learned to imitate, when the lie of the case suggested it. The last time it had happened for real had been all too recently: with Emma Pascoe. He felt the onrush of blood pressure and adrenalin that could take command of body and mind.

All his life he had been against colleagues taking casework home to their wives, though he had regularly himself ignored his own precepts. Elspeth was different: and he genuinely believed that. She had never cracked a case for him, had never even tried to pretend she had. She had never tried to interfere. There had been times, especially when he had been up against unlikely feminine quirks, when he had been glad to ask her opinion. And she had always given it objectively, sometimes with honest uncertainty. Sometimes she had been right and he had been wrong, but she had never exploited it beyond a strictly private pleasantry. It was as if, though never actually believing in masculine superiority, she had gone through all the motions of respecting it.

But now he had given her her head and see what she had made of it! Didn't she realise that this was murder they were up against? Didn't she know that this was a *case*? That the papers did not stop at Chief Superintendent level? That Top Brass, government solicitors, defence counsel would be combing out every innuendo from every sub-paragraph? That a provincial force would be watching, hyper-critical, jealous? Didn't she know that however deeply she had been involved in things, she had to be outside them at the final count?

It did not occur to Kenworthy in the heat of the moment that this might be precisely what she was trying to bring about.

What was it Menschel had said: 'let him fall in love with her for a couple of hours'?

Well, Kenworthy had known clearly enough at the time what that implied. But he had not thought that the boot was going to be on the other foot. Blast Menschel, and blast everyone else who ever monkeyed with the rules. Now Menschel's cause was served, for all the good that did anyone, and he, Simon Kenworthy, did not get a look-in.

He swung round on Elspeth. By God, this was one lesson that she'd have to learn. She was married to a copper and when you were married to a copper, there were loyalties that took precedence over some hard-luck story that you had heard from a stranger on a park-bench, even a hospital park-bench. When you were married to a copper with a reputation, that was something that you didn't put at risk for the sake of not hurting the feelings of an amiable eccentric who thought integrity meant the same thing as obstinacy.

He turned and saw Elspeth, and there was none of that loveliness, almost a bio-chemical trigger, that had saved them in the past when he had been irritated with her over some comparative trifle. She was without loveliness because she was beside herself with misery. Unhappiness and beauty were mutually exclusive. He remembered how she had described the look on Sally's face, when the news about Milner had broken.

Elspeth was full of unhappiness; but she was nowhere near to tears; she was taking too firm and well thought-out a stance for that.

He struggled to control himself, broke just about even. 'There is one man who could save this situation, if he'd only act sensibly.'

'I'd like to think, Simon, that if you were in the position that Edward Milner finds himself in, you would be behaving just as he is.'

'Aren't you getting your strings rather crossed?'

'In fact, Simon, I know you would. Always assuming that you'd let yourself get in such a spot in the first instance.

Which you wouldn't.'

The saving clause was enough, just, to hold back the flood another vital second.

'Let's get this straight,' he said. 'I'm not pumping you. I know that would be a waste of time. But I must see the shape of the record. You now know what was on this paper that the Pascoes cornered?'

'I do.'

'And it has nothing to do with a land-deal involving the Prudhoes and Sally's father?'

'That too.'

'I see. And this issue is something that the Pascoe boys understood at first sight?'

'No. They didn't know till they'd got the documents home. Tommy and Sammy never did know the whole truth. It took the old woman to see that. And she was ill-advised enough to tell Darkie.'

'I see.' Kenworthy managed to smile, conscious that it was more like a baring of his teeth, that it was nearer a grimace, the sort of cheap-jack leer he reserved for suspects, a moment before he refashioned their words into a noose for their necks. It wasn't the way he wanted to smile at Elspeth at all. He put his hand momentarily before his face, then tried again.

'In that case, I shall have to find out for myself, shan't I?'

'Yes. And you will, Simon. It will be better that way. Better for us all.'

So how illogical could a woman get?

A clever answer occurred to him. *Better for us all, you say; but don't you see that we don't count?*

He suppressed the thought. Elspeth was over-wrought. She had let herself get over-tormented by other people's sufferings, thinking in her innocence that there was something she could do about them. Well; that was Elspeth. There was no changing her. And he was damned sure he was not going to alienate her for just another case. Another forty-eight hours, and he'd have it sorted out. He went to the hall for his hat and coat.

'Where are you going?'

'Wiltshire,' he said quietly.

'It will be well after midnight, one o'clock at the earliest, before you get there.'

'People are at a low ebb when you get them out of bed in the middle of their first sleep. More amenable to wearisome repetition.'

'But what about yourself? How many broken nights have you had on the trot?'

'How much sleep do you think I shall get if I stay here?'

'You know best, Simon.' That was her most diabolical weapon. He walked to the lounge door, opened it, stood alone for a moment in the empty hall.

He knew that Elspeth had to win. It was a stupid decision he was making. And by taking away all her opposition, she had thrown it all back on to him. He came back into the room.

'They'll still be there tomorrow,' he said.

CHAPTER TWENTY

Kenworthy did leave it till tomorrow. He left it till the fag-end of tomorrow, taking Sergeant Tabrett with him with the curt announcement that there was no longer any need to maintain an Incident Office. And by the time the day was out, Sergeant Tabrett was in a position to contribute with feeling to the volume of stories that are told of Kenworthy by the men who have been out with him on assignments.

They took their time. They dropped off at Sally's hospital, taking her a packet of Turkish Delight which Kenworthy, having camouflaged it inside a carton of tissues, personally hid in her bed-side locker.

'Just to show how utterly irresponsible I am.'

They talked to her for half an hour about nothing in

particular: about a television play last night, which Kenworthy had not seen, but which he discussed with informed enthusiasm; about today's runners at Kempton, about which Tabrett found his expertise intriguing; and about the chances of a current M.C.C. tour, about which Sally's lore of averages and personalities came as an equal surprise.

'You really do take your cricket seriously, don't you?' Kenworthy asked her.

'Have to,' she answered, 'I'm not given any choice.'

But she was laughing at herself. She had clearly recovered from the worst of the shock that Elspeth had brought her, but was balanced on a knife-edge of patience waiting for the outcome. 'How much longer, Mr Kenworthy?'

'I don't know, perhaps by the time I pass this hospital again, which is likely to be in the middle of tonight. I'll drop a note in at the porter's lodge. You'll get it first thing in the morning.'

'Really?' Her face lit up in a way that made Tabrett blame him very bitterly for raising her hopes.

'No, not really,' he said enigmatically. 'But I happen to be enjoying an optimistic day, so why shouldn't you?'

'Seriously, though.'

'Seriously, I'm trying to set myself a target, just as you do when you walk three steps at physio—and pretty soon it'll be half the width of the gym, won't it?'

'By next Tuesday,' she said. 'How did you know?'

'Just by thinking hard about it. And I've been thinking hard about other things as well, about how nice it would be to get this polished off tonight.'

'And do you think you can?'

He leaned forward confidentially over her bed, having first looked round the ward for spies. 'One or two bits of information lacking, some of which I think that you can probably tell me.'

'There can't be anything about Yarrow Cross that I haven't told somebody already, two or three times, most of it. But try me out.'

'In those early days, I mean going back now to summer and Christmas 1940, when you were still getting to know Mervyn Prudhoe, how well known was all this in the village?'

'How could you keep a secret in a place like Yarrow Cross?'

'Yet I don't think your mother cottoned on in the early stages, did she? Otherwise she mightn't perhaps have come down quite so heavily when she did find out.'

'She didn't go out much, didn't meet many people. I didn't go out of my way to tell her.'

'And how about Emma Pascoe? Did she know?'

'Emma Pascoe knew everything.'

'Try and get it down to finer detail.'

And a sudden memory dawned in Sally's eyes, one of those things, forgotten since the moment of impact, that can sometimes come back years later with shattering vividness. 'It was at Christmas, the day after I'd met him on his horse. We went walking, and we met her. We ran into her along one of the lanes.'

'He had his arm round your waist?'

'God! Were you there, too? She used to wander round the countryside a lot like that, all on her own. And I can remember the odd way she looked at us, just as if I could see her now. And when we walked past her she turned round and stood still, staring at us from behind. We laughed about it, we couldn't help it. And we were a bit frightened, in case she thought we were laughing *at* her for the wrong reason, you know? But if there is such a thing as the evil eye, it was on us that afternoon. We both said the same thing.'

'Thank you, Sally. I've got it now.'

He took Sergeant Tabrett and bought him a memorable hotel lunch, spinning yarn after yarn about old cases, but steering resolutely away from this one. Throughout a sunny afternoon they ambled leisurely westwards, stopping occasionally to cast their eyes over an antique shop. They looked at village churches, Kenworthy gazing for long periods without comment at clerestories, rood-screens and, particularly, lists of vicars. He insisted on remaining at the wheel himself throughout the journey, driving with an almost maddening attention to the Highway Code, even along deserted by-roads, and sometimes not opening his mouth for an hour at a time.

'You might be thinking, Sergeant Tabrett, that I am the most monumentally patient of men, but nothing could be further from the truth. This is all but killing me. But I've had some experience of calling on farmers. And it's always a waste of time by daylight. They're out piss-hooking about their fields all day, picking blackberries and shooting rats. Or else they're off to some market, leaning over the rails for hours on end, gloating over the fleshless ribs of each other's pigs. I prefer to catch them at home.'

At first twilight he parked the car on the forecourt of an inn some twenty minutes' walk from the Prudhoes' octagonal stronghold.

'How well do you know this case, Sergeant Tabrett?'

'Tolerably well, I think, on paper.'

'Well enough to think up some pertinent but innocuous questions to ask the Prudhoes?'

'I think so.'

'Because that's what I want you to do. Keep them talking interminably about this, that and the other, until I turn up. I don't want them to be expecting me. I don't want them to know that I'm even in the neighbourhood. Least of all do I want them to guess that I'm closeted with their farm bailiff. So, their movements, their alibis, their opinions of people, tales from the hoary past ...'

'Can do,' Tabrett said. 'I'll hold the fort.'

Kenworthy paused to refresh his memory of the one-inch map, then set off down a side-road: flowering brambles, jack-by-the-hedge, the shimmering white heads of wild parsley.

He had done some pretty hefty thinking in the car; in the next few minutes he wanted to clear his mind again, to start again from scratch, to piece it all together from the initial evidence. Almost everything was clear to him now, except one crucial point: he was still uncertain who had killed Darkie Pascoe. And, how unprofessional could he be? He had to confess that the deed still mattered less to him than the history behind it.

Robert Whittle had been watching television in a dimly lit room. He came to the door blinking, recognised Kenworthy, was surprised to see him, but not excessively so. Kenworthy had just caught sight of him that night he had called on the Prudhoes, had formed no firm impression: a middle-aged man, short, spare, nothing in his expression that was strikingly good or bad, strong or weak, friendly or ill-disposed.

He led the way into a warm and well furnished farm living-room. His wife got up to leave them.

'I'd rather you stayed,' Kenworthy said. She was no Grace Pascoe, but her presence might add reality to some of the prospects that might be pending.

The room was full of military souvenirs. Kenworthy had more than half expected it: Whittle had been an active-service sergeant. A Luger, the end of its barrel plugged solid with a metallic cement, Whittle was evidently a prudent man. S.S. daggers; a bayonet to fit a standard Lee Enfield rifle; a Home Guard pike from the days when they had drilled with pick-handles.

Kenworthy unhooked a German stick-grenade from the wall, a thing rather like a policeman's truncheon, with a cylindrical war-head at its business end. He practised a few wristy tennis-shots with it.

'I take it that this thing is fool-proof immobilised?'

'Of course.'

Kenworthy looked round the collection with exaggerated concern. 'Know what I'm looking for?'

Whittle stood quite still, trying to look puzzled, not very successfully.

'A Mills 36. I'm surprised that an ex-Commando sergeant doesn't run to one of those.'

Whittle's wife moved in her chair.

'I'll tell you about that,' Whittle said.

'You'd better.'

'I took it with me when I went up there. It was a shot in the dark, really. I didn't know whether it would work or not. Delaying tactics, that was all. I certainly didn't want to hurt anyone, it *couldn't* have hurt anyone, could it?'

'That's what my colleagues and I said at the time, a gentlemanly gesture, one that happens to have wasted a lot of people's time, though.' He said this without recrimination, simply as a matter of fact.

'I just wanted to discourage interest in the well. I'd no idea that you two were going to happen along. If it had only been Darkie and Milner, it would all have worked out, and no harm done.'

'You didn't think of retrieving the stuff from the well yourself?'

'Too long a job and too risky.'

'Were you acting under direct orders?'

'No. My own initiative.'

'I suppose a Commando sergeant often anticipated. You were pretty close to Major Prudhoe during the war, were you?'

'Very.' There was a wealth of loyalty in that single word. Kenworthy avoided exploring it. 'I thought if I could only delay them, it might be ages before they could ever get into the village again. What I don't understand is what Milner wants with the stuff.'

'To protect Sally's feelings,' Kenworthy said.

'But surely she's known about it all along?'

'Known what, Mr Whittle?'

'About her father, selling up and playing a two-faced game with the village. It doesn't matter any more, does it? The older generation have nearly all passed on, and there's no resentment amongst the younger set. No one wants to go back to Yarrow Cross. Why should they?'

'That's all, is it?'

'What else could there be?'

'Nothing but land speculation in this wad of documents?'

'What else could there be?' The repetition was surely a token of sincerity.

'Didn't they tell you, either?'

'Tell me what? Who tell me?'

'The Prudhoes.'

'You've got me utterly befogged, Chief Superintendent.'

Kenworthy had to decide whether he believed this or not; he did.

'And while you're here ...'

'I'd been hoping you'd start talking in that tone of voice,' Kenworthy said.

'There's something else that puzzles me, apart from the fact that Milner doesn't seem a very likely murderer to me, especially not a knifer. And according to the newspapers, not that you can believe half you read in them, it was more or less in the old yard itself that the knifing took place.'

'More or less.'

'Very shortly after *Lights Out*?'

'Not long.'

'I planted that grenade, and I moved off into cover. And I saw you deal with it. Gutsy, that was, if you don't mind my saying so. I saw you pull out into the scrub. I heard the *Last Post*, and I must say I rather enjoyed that, it brought back a memory or two. And then I started moving out towards the perimeter. I'd like to have stayed to see what happened when Darkie and Milner arrived. You'll understand that I have relatives all over this part of Norfolk, including a mechanic at Hedges' garage, so I'd an idea what their plans were. But I also knew a fresh intake had arrived at the camp, and I didn't want to get mixed up unnecessarily in any target practice, I didn't know what their time-table was. I got out of the wire about ten minutes after *Lights Out*. And that's when Darkie Pascoe came charging past me in the dark. There was no mistaking that brute. And I'd seen a car, an Austin *Cambridge*, parked outside the perimeter, in one of the rides. I took it that it was one he'd borrowed for the evening, not necessarily with permission.'

'Well?'

'So how can he have been killed in the yard?'

'Because it wasn't Darkie that you saw,' Kenworthy said.

The truth dawned on Whittle. He had had a blind spot for this for days. '*Tommy!* I couldn't swear to it, mind you. It was too dark to see his features.'

'Did you hear him start the car?'

'Not to be sure of it. It was then that the rumpus started: your people's transport, army transport, I chose a different way out. I'd no wish to be mixed up in anything.'

Kenworthy looked towards the Whittles' telephone. 'Mind if I make a call?'

'Not much use to you, I'm afraid. This is only an extension. It's switched over to the house in the evening. I can only take incoming calls when the Prudhoes put them through.'

Kenworthy looked pensive. 'They always do seem to have had a thing about communications. The old man, anyway. He didn't seem to want a public phone in the village, if I remember.'

Whittle came somewhat unconvincingly to his defence.

'He's all right, old Prudhoe. Hasn't moved with the world, that's all. He did a lot for Yarrow Cross. But he hasn't tried to lord the manor here. Things have changed too much; it would have been one long fight. He saw that coming. I think that's why he was keen to get out of Norfolk.'

'But it's his son that you work for, isn't it?'

'One or the other of them. I've never had cause for complaint.'

CHAPTER TWENTY-ONE

Kenworthy took his time across the fields, even stopping twice to consult a pocket compass: not strictly necessary, but a comfort. And a very satisfying ingredient in the image.

In a paddock a horse came over to him, cantering spiritedly. Town-bred, he felt anything but sure of the creature's intentions. But when it came closer than he cared for, he simply shouted 'Whoa!' to it as he had seen countrymen do, and it stopped in its tracks, a mixture of habitual obedience and surprise, looking at him in the moon-light with uncertainty.

Again, he was trying to work things out from the beginning, stopped to lean against a fence in the shadows for a few minutes, cudgelling his brain.

But it was not exactly case-work that was troubling him now, not that part of it that was going to go forward on any file. He was working now on what he called *Operation Loophole*. It was gaps he was looking for, some damning inconsistency that he might have over-looked in his one-eyed reasoning.

He could find none. He would have been happier if he could have sketched it all out on a sheet of paper, to be checked and better checked and then destroyed by fire. But there was neither the light for it nor the time. He had to be satisfied with fevered cogitation, like trying to play chess without a board. He had heard of that being done.

And he could see nothing wrong in his scheme; no lurking uncover checks, no major piece suddenly won back by his opponent from the further edge of the board; no threat to his queen.

He approached the Prudhoes' neo-gothic monstrosity from the rear, along concrete paved lanes between rows of sickly white sheds, a hum of heating and ventilator motors, a stink from an air-shaft of the foetid breath of animals.

Mervyn Prudhoe let him in, limping across the chilly hall, the handle of his stick held outwards away from him. He went back to his chair, he and his father as before on either side of the great fireplace, from which issued only the heat from a single-bar electric fire. Sergeant Tabrett was sitting between them. Mervyn Prudhoe was drinking whisky, his father again a glass of white wine. Tabrett had cautiously declined refreshment; he volunteered to change his mind when Kenworthy showed no inhibition about what he was offered.

It was evident that Tabrett had succeeded in keeping his end up. An open notebook lay on his knee, a ballpoint in his hand, a page almost filled with neat, close-packed handwriting, interspersed with a ration of his own personal shorthand symbols.

Kenworthy carried his glass to the telephone. 'Mind if I use this?'

'Is it confidential?'

'No. I'd like the pair of you to hear this.'

He reached Derek at home. 'All yours from now on, Chief Inspector Stammers. I doubt whether I shall even be needed to give evidence.

'Get on to Tommy Pascoe. There is evidence available. We do know that Tommy drove his brother out to the village in a car he'd borrowed illicitly from Threeways. We do know now, at least I do, that Robert Whittle saw a figure haring away from the murder-spot towards that car. It must have been Tommy, because we do know that Darkie was otherwise engaged.

'And incidentally, I haven't checked this out yet but it can be done, you'll find that in that dash he ran pretty close to where the sheath was found.

'We could wish for better evidence. But I don't think we shall find it. It was a gloomy night, the area was a wide one, and people were not stopping to check their watches every five minutes.

'But I'm quite sure that Tommy himself will be able to fill in quite a lot of the missing detail for you. You'll have to jog his memory a little, won't you? Tell him it wouldn't have happened if Sammy had been there to stop him. Ask him what came over him when Darkie called him *Lard-head*. A good garagehand, Tommy, but not a wholly reliable member of society. He takes things too much to heart, too impulsive.'

Kenworthy paused deliberately to look round the room. It was difficult to be sure that the old man was following any of this at all. Mervyn was studying Kenworthy with an inscrutable stillness in his eyes, a stillness of concentration. Tabrett was trying to look neutrally intelligent.

Derek was talking. Kenworthy pictured him, scribbling furiously, racing to check his notes.

'Motive? Yes, Derek, it would be handy to have a motive, wouldn't it? Though I can't help thinking that when you start talking about motives and Tommy Pascoe in the same breath, you're moving about in strange country. I never think much of motives as evidence in a murder trial, though they can be fairly useful while we're still feeling our way.

'If I were you I would, again, ask Tommy. I don't think he'll be very coherent about it, but he may well say something that's significant to you and me. The trouble with Tommy is that he probably won't know his own motive, and if he does try to give you reasons, they'll likely be all the wrong ones.

'If you ask me, it all goes back to the very earliest days when the other two weren't big enough to hit Darkie back. There were seeds of hatred sown then. They flourished under his facility for involving them in his crack-brained schemes, especially when he landed them inside. And it didn't help that the old woman had a soft spot for Darkie, even when he was a mile out in the wrong. Then there was this break-in at the Prudhoes, and all this business of those papers in the well, none of which Tommy can have understood with any clarity.

'But certain things must have impinged, even on Tommy's consciousness: that the papers were important; that they held the key to a lot of money; that they meant an awful lot to Emma Pascoe; and that Darkie had done her out of them. And here was Darkie selling them out to this weird character from the R.A.F, at God knows what knock-down price. And what was Tommy's share going to be? That's one of the things you can ask him; I think he'll prove irritable on the point. And I think it was at that last moment, when he really did see that Darkie was giving away the spot to Milner, that Tommy rushed in with his knife.

'But ask him. He'll tell you.'

Kenworthy looked round the faces of the others with provocative satisfaction: Tabrett, silently agreeing with the thesis he had just heard advanced; Mervyn Prudhoe, thinking about it still, not wholly convinced, but finding no obvious flaw; the old man, to all intents and purposes indifferent.

'Oh, yes, the papers,' Kenworthy turned his face in again to the phone, as if the papers had quite slipped his mind. 'Bit of an anti-climax there, I'm afraid, Derek. A perfectly legal, but undoubtedly unpopular piece of land-conveyancing, together with some notes about the preliminary negotiations. And, incidentally, Sally's father was involved. It's understandable if Darkie put too high a price on the information. I'm a little surprised how easily he took Milner in, but we do know how credulous Milner is, don't we? Emma Pascoe made a bad mistake. She felt sure that the trading value of those documents would appreciate when the more virile elements from the village came back from the forces. Instead of which, the affair had become a dead duck. And, in any case, Darkie had gone solo with the evidence.

'No, I don't think the papers matter much. If they do come up in court, it will be as a red herring. Oh, yes, I agree, it would be as well to be ready with an account of them. The Prudhoes' solicitor must have copies. Yes. Yes, Derek, that's all. Love to Elspeth and Di.'

He put down the phone, came back only part of the way towards the others, took up an instinctive up-stage position. 'Satisfied?' he asked Mervyn Prudhoe.

'Satisfied? Why should I be satisfied? You mean that it's all over now?'

'Bar the paperwork.'

'You're relying on a confession that you haven't yet got.'

'We shall get it. As for these famous papers, Prudhoe, I suppose, in fact, that it's the original your solicitors have got.

t was very imprudent of your father to have kept copies in the house. Especially alongside certain other records.'

He did not propose to take the Prudhoes stage by stage through his reasoning. And young Tabrett could make what the hell he liked of it.

There had been elements all along that had stuck in Kenworthy's memory, though Elspeth had been told the answer before he had seen their full significance: Sally's mother, a solitary, with a strange air of distinction; a man of Mervyn Prudhoe's gallantry, apparently afraid to stand up to his father; the unexplained fact of Sally's father's freehold enclave in the heart of Prudhoe territory; and Emma Pascoe's parrot dictum, *Twice in a life-time*. He simply had not seen at the time that she was not talking about herself.

And that brought him to the other puzzle: why had Emma Pascoe insisted on waiting a few years? Why had she not cashed in there and then?

Because Emma Pascoe had seen the way that things were going; she was hoping desperately; she had met the couple on that December afternoon, had stood and stared at them, knowing what she knew. That was before the theft of the papers. When she saw the papers, she still had to wait, hoping even harder.

For the one crime which, even if committed as an honest accident, could still be used to whip up community disgust, such is the long arm of folk-guilt.

'I know what was amongst those papers,' Kenworthy said.

'You think you do?'

'A copy of a non-marriage settlement.'

But Mervyn Prudhoe was a trier to the end. 'Don't be silly, Kenworthy, this was a long time before ...'

'I mean the non-marriage settlement that your father made on Sally's mother. Home, Sergeant Tabrett. Don't forget we have a note to deliver at the porter's lodge.'

CHAPTER TWENTY-TWO

Tommy Pascoe coughed.

When he came to assemble the notes that he had taken from Kenworthy, he found that he had enough to confront Tommy with what seemed in the stress of the moment remarkably like an eye-witness account. For long minutes it had seemed as if Tommy's unreason was going to support him against persuasion. But there were details that Derek had known how to work on. Tommy had seemed strangely touched by the suggestion that things might have gone differently if Sammy had been there. When Derek mentioned the name *Lard-head*, it looked for a second as if Tommy was going to go berserk in the interrogation room.

Moreover, Tommy had an uncontrolled desire to justify himself; it impelled him to reveal things that a wiser man would have kept to himself.

His solicitor was going to rely heavily on diminished responsibility, against which the prosecution were not disposed to argue strongly. And, contrary to what a romantically-minded public might think, the ultimate colourlessness of the case did not depress the police with any sense of non-fulfilment.

Simon and Elspeth called in to see Sally on their way to start the second half of Kenworthy's leave—on the south coast, in a village where neither of them had relatives; they had last visited the place in 1940.

But they did not spend long at Sally's bedside. They saw Edward Milner, advancing down the aisle towards her bed, pushing an empty wheel-chair. Broadly smiling, clothes that looked every square inch new, brown shoes brought up to an unbelievable shine.

Unboundedly optimistic; irrational; and earnest.

Sally was going to need him.